Regards!

Bill Granger

Lake Geneva

THE
LAST GOOD
GERMAN

BOOKS BY BILL GRANGER

THE NOVEMBER MAN NOVELS

*The November Man**
Schism
The Shattered Eye
The British Cross
The Zurich Numbers
*Hemingway's Notebook**
*There Are No Spies**
*The Infant of Prague**
*Henry McGee Is Not Dead**
*The Man Who Heard Too Much**
*League of Terror**

THE MURDERS STORIES

*Public Murders**
Priestly Murders
*Newspaper Murders**
*The El Murders**

OTHER NOVELS

Time for Frankie Coolin
Queen's Crossing
Sweeps
Drover

NONFICTION

Fighting Jane (with Lori Granger)
Lords of the Last Machine (with Lori Granger)
The Magic Feather (with Lori Granger)

*Available in Warner paperback

BILL GRANGER

THE LAST GOOD GERMAN

WARNER BOOKS

A Time Warner Company

Warner Books, Inc., 666 Fifth Avenue, New York, NY 10103

W A Time Warner Company

Printed in the United States of America

First printing: November 1991

10 9 8 7 6 5 4 3 2 1

Library of Congress Cataloging-in-Publication Data

Granger, Bill.
    The last good German / by Bill Granger.
        p.   cm.
    ISBN 0-446-51552-3
    I.   Title.
    PS3557.R256L37   1991
    813'.54—dc20   91-50077
                                             CIP

For Family:
Kathy Butorac
Ruth Wellens
and my brother, John

THE
LAST GOOD
GERMAN

ONE

The flight from Washington had taken seven hours and nineteen minutes. Now a standard black Cadillac sedan was waiting for him at the curb, in a no-parking, no-stopping zone. There were no other American cars at Charles de Gaulle Airport that morning.

Devereaux stood on the walk outside the terminal for a moment, looking up at the leaden morning clouds, feeling the threat of rain in the air. Then he looked down at the Cadillac sedan, and he shook his head. It was a bad joke, all of it.

The driver got out of the car and walked around the hood to the rear passenger door and opened it.

Devereaux paused a moment before entering the car. He looked at the driver and said, "Why don't you have American flags flying on the front fenders?"

The driver blinked and said nothing.

Devereaux crawled in and dropped his bag between his knees.

The other passenger was a black man with honey-brown skin and large blue eyes. A sprinkle of freckles bridged his nose and cheeks.

"You don't appreciate our meeting you," Pendleton said.

"Not very much," Devereaux replied. The rear compartment was sealed from the driver by a bulletproof glass window. The driver had closed the door and resumed his place behind the wheel.

"You're too cautious. Everyone knows everyone in Paris. The KGB dines at Maxim's."

"I'd expect that. The Russians have bad taste in most things," Devereaux said.

"You know Paris. They said you worked here—"

"I worked here once. After Vietnam. I could speak the language," Devereaux said.

"I know all about you."

"So we know all about each other, Pendleton," Devereaux said.

Pendleton was smiling. "And?"

Devereaux said nothing.

The smile faded and the question remained unanswered. Pendleton tapped one large, manicured finger on the glass partition and the driver slipped the transmission into drive.

Flecks of rain appeared on the side windows. The air trembled with thunder from another plane taking off.

"This is really a simple matter," Pendleton said at last. The car was on the freeway out of Roissy, descending south and west toward Paris. The countryside was turning winter brown. The fields were flecked with whitewashed farmhouses with red tile roofs.

"So simple that Section sent me from Washington." Devereaux could not conceal his annoyance because the appearance of the big black Cadillac sedan had unsettled him.

He felt as naked as he had felt the night six months earlier when an operation in Albania was exposed right on the shore and he and the others had been captured. The last half a year had been full of nightmares reliving that morning on the Albanian shore, surrounded by ranks of gray-clad troops carrying AK47s. It had been over as soon as it began. Everyone was eventually killed, some more quickly than others. Everyone except Devereaux, who had been shipped to Crete as the last living witness, to tell his tale like Ishmael.

"Section wanted a fresh face on this and I agreed," Pendleton said. He was head of Paris Desk; he had helped plan the failed Albanian operation. Devereaux had been called in by Hanley in the Albanian thing. He had never met Pendleton before. He was the last man Devereaux had ever wanted to see again.

"I'm not fresh, Pendleton. I'm worn out," Devereaux said.

"It is simple, this one. This isn't Albania," Pendleton said.

"You still blame me for Albania?"

"I never blamed you or Hanley. I blame myself," Devereaux said. Closed his eyes. Saw the dead bodies, every one of them, arrayed on metal tables in a morgue in Tiranë. They made sure he had witnessed everything before they sent him back to Crete. He was a living warning of what happened to spies in Albania.

"I don't think this can be so simple."

Pendleton said, "Timing is everything in this, and I can feel it, I want it so bad. Double Eagle wants to get out and we're his best chance for that—he can see it."

"So why doesn't he drive out? You could send a Cadillac for him," Devereaux said.

Pendleton frowned. His eyes grew dark. The rain streaked wet lines on the side windows. "I don't really have to take your shit, you know," Pendleton said to the glass.

"I know. Send me home. Give me an 'unsatisfactory' for my two-oh-one file and send me home."

"I'm not going to do that, Devereaux. You've been living good off that Albania story, laying around in D.C. on 'will call' duty, just picking up your check every month."

Devereaux said nothing. Pendleton turned to look at him. "See, what you are is a man who doesn't see the possibilities. Double Eagle has two chances: slim and none. He's taking slim but he's trying to be careful. You think he'd put his own family in danger?"

"What about his family?"

"Girl named Ruth Sauer is his half sister, she's the one he's sending to Paris to check out the trail. Make sure it's safe. And that's where you come in. You go with the girl and if the Mossad ain't on your back, it's safe enough for him."

"Tell me about Mossad. Hanley didn't—"

"You don't tell Hanley everything. Not that I knew it all at first. But Mossad is after our Double Eagle and those Jews get on your case, they don't get off it. Ask Eichmann."

"Tell me about Mossad," Devereaux said again. He was feeling queasy. First, the unexpected Cadillac waiting for him. Pendleton was a sneaky bastard and he never did anything without a reason. Pendleton had been on the periphery of the Albania fiasco—brought up to speed because he was head of Paris Desk and had a finger in Europe operations—but Devereaux had not liked that part of it. Too many cooks had stirred the Albania broth. Now there was another surprise. Hanley never mentioned Mossad.

"Mossad has made a connection of Kurt Heinemann to the massacre back a couple of years ago. At the Olympic games in Munich, you remember what I'm talking about?"

Devereaux stared at the rolling brown countryside. He remembered France as full of rainy days like this, just wet and cold enough to be melancholic. Or maybe that was always his mood and the countryside did its best to reflect the inner man.

"When Al-Fatah killed those eleven Israelis in Munich in 1972, Israel went after Syria and Lebanon. Bombed shit out of the Arabs. That was openers. They wanted to find out how the terrorists worked it, got into Germany, got into the Olympic Village. They knew there had to be a German connection. They figured on Bonn but Bonn broke its ass for Tel Aviv and eventually Mossad saw who the German was. An East German boy working as a terrorist for Stasi code-named Double Eagle. Our boy, Kurt Heinemann. Kurt Heinemann has real trouble, Jews on his ass. They think he set up Al-Fatah with everything they needed and they want him very bad."

"Do we know this or is this the story that Kurt Heinemann is peddling to you?"

Pendleton started to say something and then stopped. He stared out his side window. "Fucking rain. Six straight days we haven't seen the sun."

"It's still there," Devereaux said.

Silence. The tires thumped over the pavement, sending up a perpetual trail of rain clouds behind.

"I know some things and I don't know other things. I picked up this Mossad stuff in the last week. We got informers, they got informers, all God's chillun got informers. They see, I see, we all see. I pick up this Mossad stuff from a man who knows a man who is the brother of the day bartender at Harry's who is the friend of a friend. Look. I run my desk. I tell Hanley what I absolutely know. I don't absolutely know about Mossad, which is why I don't tell him."

Devereaux stared at the bag between his knees. He had stored it all these months on the top shelf of his spare closet. He had never wanted to go anywhere again. They gave him pills to let him sleep; when he slept the drugged sleep, he dreamed of dead bodies naked on metal tables in a Tiranë basement. He had known them all.

"So he's sending his sister out as bait," Devereaux said.

5

"And I'm supposed to go along with her to find Kurt Heinemann."

"Kurt Heinemann is gonna find you. He's gonna see there ain't no Mossad on his trail and then he's gonna come up to the Rue Scribe and turn his sorry ass over to me."

"And what if Mossad wants him?"

"Tough tit."

"We wash hands with Mossad."

"But we're top dog and when we piss out our territory, Mossad knows when to stop sniffing it."

"So I'm a setup, is that it, Pendleton?"

Silence. No gloom, just a small fire of animosity sparked between the two men.

"You wait for her every morning for a week starting tomorrow at the Gare de l'Est. Wait for the Zurich train in the morning. That shouldn't be too hard."

"I want a piece," Devereaux said.

"For what? You gonna shoot this girl? This girl is a schoolgirl, she's only seventeen."

"And how old is Kurt Heinemann?"

"He ain't gonna shoot you."

"He wants to come to Uncle. How do you know that?"

"I know things. That's what we do in Paris Desk. We know things and sometimes we know important things."

It was wrong, it was all wrong; it was like falling, it was the smell of that Albanian beach on that morning; it was false and wrong and everyone knew it but no one could say anything. They were sleepwalking to death and they knew it and none of them could pull back.

Christ. Devereaux shivered and Pendleton saw it. Devereaux's face was the color of chalk and his gray eyes were bleak. He saw things past; he saw things coming.

TWO

C *afé au lait et pain et beurre,"* Devereaux said. The waiter brought the milky coffee and the buttered pieces of bread and left a saucer with a printed bill.

Rain again.

The dirty streets around the station were choked with traffic and the fumes of Gauloises mixed with diesel exhaust.

He had been at the station every morning since the first meeting with Pendleton. They had made no further contact. Pendleton had put him up at a nice hotel on the Champs-Elysées; he had moved out within three hours of registration and found a bare room in a one-star hotel near the station. On the second afternoon in Paris, he had purchased a 9mm automatic from a fence in the rue de Verneuil on the Left Bank, a man he had used before on his first assignment. Three days after that, Devereaux made a signal to Hanley in Washington. It was a locator signal, nothing more, and it

7

told Hanley only that Devereaux was still alive and still in the field and still in deepest black. Nothing more. He didn't want to use the safe phone in the rue de Scribe at Section offices. He didn't want to deal with Pendleton at all.

Devereaux sat in a different café near the station every morning. He sat by the window and he watched the pedestrians and loiterers, the clochards with their rags and sense of proprieties eyeing the other citizens like marks waiting to be scored. He watched for people who might be watching him.

On the third morning, he had spotted the watcher in the shadow of the entrance of the ornate Gare de l'Est. The watcher had followed him down the platform to meet the Zurich train. The girl had not been on the train. Pendleton had said she would wear a blue melton coat and there were always girls getting off the train and there were women in blue coats but Devereaux was sure that Ruth Sauer had not arrived in Paris. He was sure about the watcher as well; the man was following him.

So Devereaux had let the watcher follow him down a tangle of narrow streets away from his hotel. When he found the street he wanted, Devereaux slipped into a shadowed entrance and waited. When the watcher came abreast of him, Devereaux put the muzzle of the automatic against his forehead. Just that suddenly and painlessly.

"Jesus Christ," the watcher said.

"Who do you work for?"

"You know," the watcher said. "Jesus Christ."

"Not Jesus Christ," Devereaux said.

"Pendleton."

"Is that true? The best thing is to finish you and not guess about whether you're telling the truth."

"I'm Section, Section." Rain glistened on his forehead; maybe it was sweat as well.

"Tell him to leave me alone," Devereaux said.

"You checked out of the hotel—"

"And tell him I have a gun and tell him to stay out of my way," Devereaux said. "And don't ever go to the Gare de l'Est again."

"I won't," the watcher said.

"Good."

"Can I go?"

"Yes."

The watcher had scurried away, looking behind him once or twice, but by then Devereaux had slipped out of the shadowed door and into another street.

The girl came on November 3.

She truly was a girl. She was slim and the coat seemed bulky on her body. She carried a single bag. Her hair was brown, cut short. She had large brown eyes.

Devereaux kissed her on the platform. They embraced as friends or lovers. She let the kiss linger. It was a kiss of greeting and sign of recognition: I am who you think I am. But what else was there in the kiss? Devereaux let the kiss linger also and he was puzzled by the urgency of her slim body. Who was this girl really? Was any of this true?

"I'm sorry I made you wait so long," she said. Her voice was very deep for one so young and slight. There was softness in it and the trace of an accent. "My brother is so careful."

"I'm careful too."

"What is your name?"

"November," he said.

"Yes. That's the name," she said. "Are you sure of me?" A rare smile then; not at all shy.

He had to smile. "You're the only pretty girl in a blue coat. I'm sure of that."

"Did they say I was pretty?"

"Perhaps," Devereaux said. He felt awkward. She was very young and he felt attracted to her—by the force of that

9

kiss, by the press of that young body against him—and he felt ashamed of himself. And, for that moment, he had lost the sense of danger. That frightened him most of all.

He resumed his frown. "Let's go. I'll take your bag."

"Is it far?"

"Not very far."

"Is it a nice hotel?"

"Not very nice."

"I always thought of Paris. And coming here to a beautiful hotel and eating beautiful food."

"We can get the food at least."

"Not now." She hugged at his arm as he led her down the platform to the concourse. Birds flew back and forth from ledge to ledge across the ceiling. The doors to the street were open. Traffic pounded against the rain-swept streets, creating chaotic noises. She held his arm very tight and stopped. She looked at the Paris she had dreamed about over storybooks; it was gray, rather shabby, very loud. Disappointment colored her eyes a deeper brown and Devereaux saw it all in that instant and pitied her.

"The sun shines too," Devereaux said.

She gave him that smile. "And the food is good," she said.

"Very good."

"I ate on the train. It wasn't very good. I felt sick from the train," she said. Again, the voice was deep, melting, too experienced to come from that youthful face and those lips. "I'd like to lie down."

"The room has a single bed," he said.

She looked at him. "I don't care," she said.

Again, the sense of danger left him. He tried to drag it back. He felt the weight of her arms wrapped around his arm. What did he expect her to be anyway?

The Hotel du Monde had a glass door and a century of stained stones piled to a height of six stories. He led her past the concierge's desk. The concierge was a fat man with a waxed mustache who read the racing news all day. He looked up, saw the girl, glanced at Devereaux, then made a shrug and turned to the results from l'Auteil.

The carpeted stairs creaked. The fourth level was a narrow corridor that led into an adjoining building. The room was at the end. The door was flimsy and did not set exactly against the jambs. Devereaux turned the key in the lock and opened it. He led her into their room.

The wallpaper was covered with brown flowers that might have once been other colors. The bed was made up, wide and with a sag in the middle. The room had a washstand with thin towels on a metal rod and a bidet. There was a set of window doors opened to the noise of the street, and the rain.

"Do you want me to close the windows?"

"I like to hear the rain," she said. "I'm tired but it's just a little tiredness from the train. Just let me take a little sleep, November."

"A little sleep," Devereaux repeated, staring at her. She had shrugged off her coat. Her dress was also covered with dull flowers, faded from another time. It was a woman's dress on a girl's body.

"I'm eighteen years old," she said. "My brother trusts me to be his eyes for him. To see if it is safe."

"I don't know if it's safe."

"Who does know?"

"No one," Devereaux said.

"That is very honest of you," she said. She stood still, letting him watch her. Neither moved. Thunder bowled down narrow streets and rattled the tall window doors. "What we do is we take a train. And we just go to some place where Kurt can see that we are not followed."

"Who is following Kurt?"

"He is in great danger always," she said.

"And he puts you in harm's way."

11

"No. We have no danger, you and I." Again, she let the teasing smile linger. Then she took a step toward him. She touched his sleeve.

"Are you afraid of anything?" Ruth said.

"Everything."

"Then why do you do this?"

"It's what I do."

"Don't you have comfort? Your wife? Or lover?"

"There are lovers," he said. Why was he answering her questions? But he knew. The weight of her light touch was a thousand pounds. In a moment, the tension would have to be broken, one way or another. The door was closed, the windows open, and the room was empty of witnesses, time, or even place.

"I want a little sleep," she said. She kissed him then, with the same wet force she had greeted him with on the platform. So unexpected. She reached her arms around him and pulled his head down into the kiss so that he would not have escaped it even if he had wanted to. "Can you bring me bread? A little of the French bread and cheese?"

She pulled away.

Devereaux again tried to drag back the sense of danger but danger had fled the earth. What the hell did it matter now?

"All right," he said.

He turned to the door. "Don't answer any knock," he said, turning to her.

"There's no danger."

He stared at her. She had confirmed it. There was no danger anymore in the world as long as they stayed together in this room on this rainy day.

THREE

He had left bread and cheese on the table by the bed and stared at her sleeping. Then he had left as quietly as he entered. He had gone into the streets and set up a trail to see if there were followers.

He walked all over Paris in the rain. The rain was lighter now and it just wet his face and he could have wiped it away with the palm of his hand.

He did not come back until after midnight and she was waiting for him. She had been reading a book. She had removed her dress and sat in bed in a small white bra, covered by the blanket to the waist. She had glanced up when he entered and put the book on her lap.

"I thought you might not be coming back."

"I was making a trail. To see if anyone was following it."

"You're very careful, aren't you?"

"No. I just don't like this."

"What don't you like? Me?"

"I mean, I don't like this." He went to the open window. The rain had stopped. The night was still and it smelled sweet because the rain had cleansed the world. The light from the single bulb was dim and the shadows in the room were huge.

"Why don't you get in bed with me and we can talk."

"I don't want to sleep with you," Devereaux said. But he didn't look at her. He stood at the window and looked down the narrow street to the place where the prostitute stood every night under the streetlamp and to the other place where the clochard pitched his mattress each evening. The clochard had found some place indoors; so had the prostitute. "I want to know where Kurt is."

"Kurt is where Kurt is. He wants to see that you have a clean trail."

He turned and looked at her. "I don't believe you."

"I'm really who I say I am," she said.

"Why do you want to make love then? Why are we here? Why don't we go and find Kurt?"

"He'll find us, I told you. If you want to go, then we can leave tomorrow night. We take the overnight train to Zurich."

"You came to Paris to pick me up and take me back to Zurich with you? This is absurd," Devereaux said. He shook his head. No worry about finding danger now. It was in the room, in the shadows, waiting on the street, under the bed. In the body of the young woman with small breasts and a boyish haircut and large brown eyes.

"It is not absurd," she said. "You're the conductor for safe passage. When it is safe, Kurt will know. And you take him safe to America."

"I take him safe to the rue de Scribe," Devereaux said.

"And I tell you what Kurt tells me to do," Ruth said in that final way that Germans have.

He was alone. He had not liked or trusted Pendleton. He had separated himself and gone into black and purchased a pistol on the illegal market. He had threatened a Section watcher on the street. All right, he had cut himself off and now he was talking to a German schoolgirl who might be death incarnate. He realized he was fingering the trigger guard of the automatic in his coat while he looked at her.

"Kurt is in danger." Softer in tone. "He would not ask me to do this except for the danger. The Jews want to kill him."

"Because he helped to kill the Jews."

She stared at him. There. Just a glimpse of it in the large brown eyes. Devereaux felt reassured by the hatred he saw flame up.

"He is what you are. A spy does for his country."

"So they say."

"Did you ever kill anyone?"

Let me think. The first was a boy in Thailand with a bomb in his trousers. The second was . . . who was the second? The third. Devereaux closed his eyes. Dead bodies on metal tables with bullet punctures and slit throats. Opened his eyes.

"I take you to Zurich. If it is right, then Kurt will go with you to America."

"What will you do?"

"I will go home."

"Where is home?"

"In Leipzig."

"Kurt lives in Leipzig?"

"Kurt lives in many places. Home is in Leipzig."

"Mother? Father?"

"My father was Otto Sauer. He is dead. Kurt's father was Ernst Heinemann and he is dead too. He is dead in America. Kurt was a little boy in America and when his father is dead, my mother—our mother—goes home. To Leipzig."

"In the German Democratic Republic."

15

"It is hard sometimes but it is good, life is good." Said with the German stamp of approval.

"So you're a good communist."

"I am what I am," she said.

"What are you, Ruth?"

"I am his sister," she said. "That's what I am." She stared at him. "You do not have to be so hard to me. I am only his message to you. He does not trust, you do not trust, you are alike. I cannot think how anyone can live with so many doubts."

"Why do you want me to sleep with you?"

A question. It hung in the still air of the midnight room.

"Do I have to say?"

Devereaux released the grip of the pistol in his pocket. "Go to sleep, Ruth. In the morning, we can talk about where to go."

"What will you do?"

"Nothing. Take a walk. Breathe the night air. The rain has stopped."

"Don't leave me," she said. "I am not so brave."

And he saw it was true.

He went to her and sat down next to her on the bed and he put his arms around her and held her. Then he pulled the cover up to her chin.

"Don't leave me," she said.

"No," he said.

He sat on the bed and watched her until she fell asleep. Then he crossed to the windows and pulled up a single straight chair. He took off his shoes and put his stockinged feet on the window ledge and looked at the narrow landscape of the city street. He sat and, after a while, he dozed. Without dreams this time. He would awaken and shake his head and then doze again. In this way he spent the rest of the night. He was not aware of her in the moments when she woke up and stared at him for a long time before falling asleep again.

During the day, he bought her croissants and cafés and they went to the Louvre. The day was bright and crisp and Paris was as beautiful as a storybook drawing.

The train left the Gare de l'Est at 11:30 each evening. She held his arm and he carried both bags. They paid for a compartment on the half-empty train and the wagons-lits attendant took their passports and promised to wake them just before they arrived in Zurich at six in the morning. He would see they were not disturbed and the passports were stamped at the Swiss border.

"We won't be disturbed," she said to him once they closed the door of the compartment. "And there is no chair for you to sit in."

He smiled at her. She had toured Paris with a heart-breaking enthusiasm that stirred Devereaux. This couldn't be all fake. He wanted to keep his edge because there was something so wrong about this but she kept blunting the edge with her smiles and little hugs and large-eyed wonder as she toured the stately rooms of the art museum. She overwhelmed him.

"I'm going to stand outside," Devereaux said.

"Are you afraid of me?"

"No. Outside the train until we leave. Just to watch the trail," he said.

When he returned the express was rocketing through the eastern suburbs into the French countryside. The night was clear and the bright moonlight painted ghostly fields. He waited in the corridor of the sleeping car for a while, expecting anything. And then he could not wait any longer.

She was in the top bunk, covered to her neck with blankets.

He took off his trousers and shirt and hung them on the door. He slipped into the lower bunk in his shorts.

He lay there with his eyes open and he thought about the girl above him.

He expected it.

Her naked foot was on the ladder and then she stood a moment beside the lower bunk before she pulled down her white panties. He touched her naked belly with his hand; he could not see her face above the bunkline. She pressed her small, slightly rounded belly against his hand and he rubbed her there in slow circles. She took his hand; he still could not see her face. She put his hand between her legs and he felt her there and felt the wetness. She made a sound then that was the sound of wanting and contentment at the same time.

The compartment was locked but doors could be forced. He thought about the pistol in the pocket of his coat hanging on the door. Put the pistol beneath the pillow. Be prepared.

She bent over him and then crawled into the lower bunk. She kissed him, her hands behind his head, pressing herself against him on the covers and licking at his tongue with her tongue.

Security. An agent could crash the door in five seconds with the right pick. Or use the attendant's key, explain the couple were wanted in connection with a robbery . . .

"Take those off," she whispered. The voice was really a growl by now and he pushed down his shorts. She touched him, held him in her right hand, and then she bent over him and took him in her mouth. She made another sound.

The train rocked back and forth through the night. The moon made shadows beneath trees and farm fences and hedgerows. The train was sealed like a secret. The blue nightlight in the compartment only made the darkness more visible.

She lifted her mouth back to his lips and he wanted her

very much. He moved over her and was between her legs and he let her lap feel the weight of his body settle on her. She groaned now but there was so much hunger in it that it sounded like a roar to him.

They made love.

After they made love, she told him about Kurt. She said that Kurt was a good man who loved his country and his mother and his half sister and took care of them. He could even arrange for Mother to shop in the special stores. He would come back from Moscow with furs for them but Mother never wore her fur hat because she did not want to assume airs. Mother had buried two husbands in two different countries and she had known all the horrors of modern times, from the time of the war to the Russian liberation to the refugee camps . . .

Everything she said could be a lie, Devereaux thought, except there was too much.

They made love again after they both awoke from a light sleep. They made love more slowly. Ruth Sauer wanted this and then that and he gave them to her. She asked him what he wanted and he did not say it in words but she felt the pressure of his hands and his body and she gave those things to him that he wanted.

They were asleep in each other's arms when the attendant knocked at the door. They rose like guilty people and dressed apart, not looking at each other.

The attendant brought them their stamped passports and coffee and croissants. The croissants were large, flabby Swiss ones and the coffee was ordinary, not at all like coffee in Paris.

The *Bahnhof* bustled, even at six in the morning. Trains were launched across Europe from this place. Cheerful Swiss newspapers with gaudy red headlines crammed the stands next to even gaudier German papers and sober gray sheets from Britain. The world bustled inside the concourse; outside, the city was still dozing beneath the clocktower of Saint Peter and the Alpine peaks all around.

"Where do we go now?"

Ruth looked at him. They had left their bags in the left luggage. She seemed different now because she had broken him down, penetrated, made him surrender suspicions even for a little while in a locked compartment on an overnight train.

"There's a place we go in the old town," she said. "Come on."

"We can take a taxi—"

"No. We must walk. Maybe Kurt is watching us now, watching the trail—"

Devereaux felt absurd and exposed again. Of course Kurt could be watching. So could Mossad. So could KGB and anyone else who might want to kill a German terrorist about to defect. Or capture an American spy. What would Hanley say when Devereaux disappeared into Lubyanka prison in Moscow? What would Pendleton explain in his report but that Devereaux went into black against instructions and it was no business of Pendleton's from then on?

They walked down the Bahnhofstrasse toward the lake. The dawn was drab because the sun takes a long time to rise above mountains. The dingy air did not conceal the glitter of the street. So many watches and furs and rich people's things were arrayed behind thick glass displays.

"How can you go home?" The thought had nagged him from the first.

"I am nothing," she said. "Not Stasi, not nothing. Nothing will touch me, we are Germans after all, not barbarians like the Rumanians. If Kurt must go to America, he must go to America."

"But you don't want to go."

"I am a German."

"I don't understand you. Any of this."

She stopped and looked at him and held both his arms on her hands. "I am what I am."

"What are you?"

"I do this for Kurt, except I make love to you for me. That was mine. You are pretty, November. You have cold eyes but they are clear and your teeth are pretty. I felt your arm and it was very strong and then you said you were not careful, only afraid. Only a strong man can say he is afraid. So I wanted to see you naked and to feel how you could make love to me. That is all this is. That is honest. Kurt is honest. He must become safe and he does what he must. That is all, November; life is not so complicated." She smiled in the way of women smiling at foolish men.

They walked all the way to the Zuricher Zee. The swans were nestling in the water at the retaining wall. Drug addicts were smoking on the bridge, living off their highs of the evening. The druggies watched the girl and the man pass them. Devereaux looked into every face.

They went into the tangle of old streets and walked in the middle of the road because the streets were so narrow and because Devereaux did not want to be close to shadowed entrances. He gripped the pistol in his coat and flicked the safety. She seemed not to hear the click.

A small wooden sign: GASTHAUS.

She took a key out of her pocket.

Devereaux wet his lips. He was trusting her and that was stupid, all of it was stupid from the fat Cadillac at the airport to this place on a Zurich morning.

The key led to a courtyard to a narrow entrance at the back and an unlocked door. The door led into a corridor full of more doors. She used another key on another door at the end of the corridor and opened to a large, windowless room.

There was a bed with a featherbed on it and a dresser without a mirror. She turned on the wall light and illuminated the room.

"Now we wait," she said.

"For what?"

"For Kurt."

She closed the door. The lock clicked. A room without windows, typical of rooms behind the garish clubs of the redlight district. Rooms for prostitutes and their customers, without a view but with a modicum of privacy.

She said, "I would like to make love to you again."

"Your brother might walk in." He waited.

She bit her lip. "He might walk in," she said.

So she didn't know. Devereaux watched her thinking about it. Now she really was a girl again, thinking about an illicit rendezvous with a stranger, thinking about how to get away with it. It reassured him in that moment. Maybe everything was true.

He thought that as the door burst open.

Two men in stocking masks.

Uzis.

He registered this and fired through his coat.

The second man grabbed Ruth by the throat and she screamed.

The bullet struck the first man in the face and it exploded in the confines of the nylon stocking like a tomato dropped on concrete.

The second man pushed Ruth on the bed and turned the Uzi toward Devereaux just as Devereaux fired twice more. The Uzi sputtered a streak across the ceiling, smashing plaster into snow. He was dead as he hit the floor and Ruth was screaming and couldn't stop.

He grabbed her arm and still she couldn't stop. He slapped her hard.

She stared at him.

"Where's Kurt?" he said.

"I don't know—"

He hit her, and not to stop her screaming. He hit her to hurt her. She flinched and he hit her again. His eyes were colored by the killing. Two men dead and he could smell the powder in the room and his eyes glittered because of the killing.

"Where is he?"

"He told me to wait here, he told me—"

"You fucking liar," Devereaux said. He looked at the dead men. KGB or Mossad, what did it matter, this was some kind of a setup and he was the stooge and she was the lure and—

Her nose was bleeding. Blood on her teeth. She wiped at it and there were tears in her eyes. "They were going to kill us," she said.

Maybe it was true.

He saw his hand was shaking even though it held the pistol. He was feeling it as suddenly as deceleration from a high speed, feeling the pressure on his face and kidneys. He wanted to beat her until she told him the truth but there were dead men on the floor.

He grabbed her arm and pulled her roughly over the bodies and through the open, splintered door. The corridor was empty.

"Come on," he said. He half dragged her down the corridor.

"We have to wait—"

He turned to her then.

Which was why he didn't see the opening door behind him.

Didn't even feel the blow except to see black expanding from the edges of her wide-eyed, innocent face as he crumpled to the floor.

FOUR

Eyes open.

Devereaux struggled up. In bed. Same windowless room. Dead bodies.

Ruth. Ruth was gone.

Stared at the bodies.

Then saw the man in the chair with the Uzi.

A small white scar from the left temple to the ear. Narrow face, high cheekbones, black eyes. Burning black eyes and short, brown, spiky hair.

Devereaux wet his lips with a dry tongue. "Kurt Heinemann," he said.

"*Ja, ja,*" Kurt Heinemann said. A thin smile. "You hurt Ruth."

"Your sister."

"*Ja,* my sister."

"And I fucked her."

The smile faded until the face was completely neutral except for the eyes that could melt steel.

"Who were they?"

"Mossad," Kurt Heinemann said. "I didn't expect you to kill them for me but I thank you. I only wanted them to find me in a place and a time of my choosing. Mossad killed by an American agent. It is wonderful. I thank you very much."

"You sold Pendleton a load of bullshit."

"No. It is true that Mossad is after me but this will hurt them very badly. These were good men, both of them. They thought you were meeting me and they might have killed you. In any case, you killed them. No, I only sell the blackie a half of a load of bullshit. I am not ready to become an American just yet, Devereaux."

Devereaux caught it; he knew the name, not the code name. What the hell was going on?

"I don't want you to die just yet even if you make love to my sister."

"Is she really your sister?"

"You were so suspicious of her that you forgot about me."

"She sold me but at least I got her to suck me off," Devereaux said. He was waiting and watching the muzzle of the Uzi.

Kurt let the neutral face fall into a frown. "I don't like that talk."

"We didn't talk a lot. We just did it."

"But I won't kill you, Devereaux. You see?"

"I'd kill you."

"But that's the difference. You've done me the great favor of killing Mossad. I want you to take the credit for it. And then you can explain how you were fooled by the Double Eagle again. It's a good joke on R Section. And the blackie in Paris, he can explain how he was fooled."

Ishmael again. He would be the witness against himself,

the witness from Albania transformed into the witness in a whorehouse in Zurich.

"Ruth fooled me," he said.

"*Ja, ja,* believe that even if it is not true. Ruth did not understand what I wanted to do. Not about you, about them. Ruth can only tell you the truth."

"Where is she?"

"In a car going home. I send her home with Hans and she says I should not hurt you. I should cut off your balls for what you told me. She is eighteen years old. You are really a swine."

"And you're a Nazi pimp. You use your sister like a two-dollar whore, you Jew-killing bastard," Devereaux said in a soft voice, a voice without any edge to it except in the content of the words.

"No, Devereaux. You killed the Israelis, not me. You did me a service."

Devereaux decided he wouldn't wait any longer. He rolled from the bed and Kurt Heinemann stood up as he hit the floor. Devereaux rose with coiled quickness, the kind of karate move they taught the agents in Japan before shipping them with the other advisors into Vietnam. It almost worked.

Kurt staggered back from the kick blow but held the Uzi and fired a single shot. The bullet caught Devereaux in the chest; it spun him around and slapped him to the floor.

Kurt took two steps to the body curled against the wall.

"Goddamnit," he said in clear English. He pushed at Devereaux to see his chest and see the wound. Devereaux's eyes were rolling back in his head. "Don't you die yet, you bastard," Kurt Heinemann said.

He went into the corridor and looked at his watch. Eight A.M. and the bastard was late; it was running behind, all of it. For a moment he felt panic. And then he took a deep breath and let the calm spread over him. Minutes ticked and he didn't count them. Waited. Heard a moan from the bedroom. Devereaux dying.

And then the man he waited for filled the doorway to the courtyard at the end of the hall of doors.

"You're late," Kurt Heinemann said, training the Uzi on the other man.

"Or you were too early," the large man said. "What happened?"

"Mossad. He finished them off."

"Boy got himself a gun. Told him he didn't need one."

"He did me a favor," Kurt Heinemann said. "Then I had to shoot him."

"Is he dead?"

"No. And you get him help."

"Why should I?"

"You dumb bastard, what do you think? Devereaux is the stooge for this. Otherwise, they will strip your black ass."

Pendleton said, "All right, Kurt. I see what you mean. But where's part two?"

Kurt stared at him for a moment and then went down the long, empty corridor to the black man standing in the courtyard door. Kurt made a face that was an inaudible snarl and took the paper from his pocket.

Pendleton looked at the list. Ten names in ten places; ten similar occupations.

"This is good shit," Pendleton said. He folded the list and put it in his pocket. He smiled a broad smile. "I don't get you, Kurt, I really don't. You could come home to Uncle and we'd treat you better than you have been treated. You give me a list of ten Russian agents in my bailiwick just like that, but you won't come over to my side."

"Russians," Kurt said.

"Beg pardon?"

"You never understand. Those are Russians. I do not work for Russians."

"Yeah, yeah, you work for Stasi which is a stooge for the KGB."

A small smile of pure contempt crossed Kurt Heinemann's thin, scarred face. Pendleton saw it, even understood it. Pendleton shook his head.

"Auf wiedersehen," Kurt Heinemann said in a flat voice. "We may do business again."

Pendleton stared at him with those cold, blue eyes set in the glowing brown face.

"I am sorry you have to sacrifice your agent," Kurt said. He was in no hurry.

"November is not as important as this, this list. You had a problem with Mossad, I use November to take care of it for you. And we both don't leave a trail so there's no connection of you to me or me to you. November was our . . . necessary loss, you might say."

"It is the way of things. Soldiers get used," Heinemann said, still waiting, still trying to fathom the man he was dealing with.

"You might come over to our side sometime."

"I don't think so, Herr Pendleton. Maybe I do what I do because . . ." He paused. What should he say?

Pendleton grinned. "Because you're a patriot, right? God and Lenin bless the GDR. Yeah, the last good German, ain't you?"

Heinemann did not understand the smile. It was a smile of contempt and he resented it but he did not understand it. What did Pendleton believe in then? What was this game to him then?

And he thought he should leave now, before the grinning American began to speak again.

FIVE

Moscow had depressed Kurt Heinemann deeply. The gloom was gathered in the stones, in the dreary apartment building walls, in the darkness of the Kremlin streets, in all the conference rooms. The conference was over at last, the last rumors were repeated in the special clubs inhabited by off-duty KGB officers, and Kurt Heinemann could not wait to escape the dread that was everywhere in Moscow.

He had learned everything informally. He had longstanding friends inside KGB and they told him things they would not repeat inside the walls of KGB headquarters. They told him what he had suspected; that it was just dawning on them, on the Russian insiders, chilled him because they were so far behind in their own intelligence. They spoke like children of the change happening all around them. They said they feared Moscow was going to let loose the reins, let the Warsaw Pact disintegrate, that the mobs making demonstra-

31

tions in places like Leipzig and East Berlin and Bucharest and Sofia . . . well, the mobs would have their way and they could scarcely believe it. They wanted to cling to something but they didn't know what it was. They were deluding themselves and that made the depression so much worse.

Kurt Heinemann could not wait to change planes in Berlin for Leipzig, to shake off the Russian mentality he had spent ten days understanding. Only one of the Russians he knew had been cleared-eyed enough to see the end of the world: "We will hang on to ourselves, Kurt, only ourselves, and the rest of the world will be let to drift out to sea. The GDR will be no more, Kurt. You must escape this. You must come into Moscow. We will make it safe for you."

A pension in Moscow. Live like a Russian for the rest of his days. It had frightened him, to think of it. The end of the world was coming to Moscow too and the fools didn't even see it.

The Interflug flight to Leipzig was as dreary as a flight on a Russian-built plane could be but Kurt did not notice his discomfort. He merely wanted to be among Germans again, to see if the madness infecting the world could be contained by rational thought, rational acts. He could scarcely hide his contempt for the Russians anymore; they had gained half the world and were now letting it slip away because they did not know how to make enough bread for peasants.

He took his own car from Leipzig airport to his mother's home. He needed to be in his mother's home now, he needed the reassurance of its familiar smells and familiar talk. He needed his mother's frank assurance that the world would not end after all.

There were crowds on the streets. Slogans and banners. Drunken youths. Broken shop windows. Surges of people in unexpected places. Madness, madness.

He entered his mother's house and it was calm except for the drone of the television set. She watched the news and the news told her nothing of the crowds she had seen with her own eyes that day. She kissed her son when he entered the half-darkened living room at the front of the modest brick house and they watched the news on television together, in silence. When it was over, without a single truth having been told, she turned the set off. They sat together in silence.

"What do they say in Moscow?" she finally said. She was a vigorous woman in her seventies and she still shopped every day on foot exactly like a peasant, though Kurt had offered her a car and a driver. He shared her stubborn countenance and clear black eyes.

"They say one thing in one place and a different thing in another place," he said. "It is very bad now. Bad."

"For you." A statement.

He sighed and rose and went to the sideboard. He poured himself a small brandy schnapps. He tasted it and then put it down on the sideboard with his back to her.

"Where is Ruth?"

"She went out to see the crowds."

"That's foolish, Mama. She could be hurt."

"I told her. She laughed and said that no one would dare to hurt the sister of the Double Eagle."

"*Ja.* The Double Eagle. Invincible."

Bitter.

She turned in her rocker and looked at him. "What will you do?"

"What can I do? If everything is gone then I'm gone."

"There are no police in the streets. There was a water cannon yesterday but not today. The mobs break windows."

"Mobs always break things," Kurt Heinemann said. "I can go to Moscow. To be safe."

"Will you go to Moscow?"

"No. I couldn't breathe there. And what about you, Mama?"

"I don't care. My life is long and almost over. *Ja*, it's true, *Liebchen*. But I don't care for me. I care for you. You are in danger. And what can Ruth do now without you?"

"Ruth, Ruth."

They said her name like that very often. Ruth, Ruth. A strange girl grown into a strange woman. She worked very well for long periods—she was a teacher in more than one school—and then she would have to go away inside herself. She would take a lover and live with him and then it would be over and she would come to Kurt to arrange things. There had been two abortions. And once, Kurt had to kill a man who insisted about Ruth. Ruth didn't want them for very long, just for a while, just for some fantasy that she could not explain.

He had thought about it in Moscow in all the dreary days and nights conferring with his colleagues inside KGB. He had already begun to plan his escape before he realized he would have to escape. And he had thought about his sister in exactly that tone of voice: Ruth, Ruth. Wearily said. Sadly said. Shaking his head when he said it. He loved her very much and she loved him. She had once tried to make love to him as she made love to her men and he had been horrified and that had made her crazy for weeks after; she had fits of weeping and she would moan in her bedroom at night. Ruth, Ruth.

"I have to go away," he said to his mother. A clock on the mantel ticked off unseen minutes. The house was very still, very calm, the center of the stormy world. "I will take Ruth with me."

"Where can you go?" Softly, waiting for the answer with dread.

"You know," he said to her back.

She gazed out the window and held her breath. Then she shook her head. "*Ja*, Kurt. I know. Will they harm you?"

"They will welcome me. I can bring them my mind. There

was a contact. Many contacts with them. But one I have in mind. He is very important now. I can use him if he thinks he can use me."

"Can he be trusted?"

"Not at all. It's all right. I can't be trusted either."

"That dreadful place," she said.

It was her word for America, where she had buried one husband. She would never say the name of the country; it was only "that dreadful place."

"*Ja, ja.* For some while. If the country falls, then the Stasi will be torn apart. I will take care of myself. And Ruth. But what can I do for you?"

"Leave me," she said. "Children have to save themselves."

"Mama." And there were tears in the hard, bright eyes that she could not see because she was looking out the window at the empty street. "I love you, Mama."

"I love you, son. But take care of Ruth, that's what must be done."

"It'll be done," he said.

"I love you," his mother said.

They repeated the phrase in the semidarkness of the still house. They repeated the mantra several times when silence threatened to overwhelm them. They waited for Ruth to come home and were relieved when she did. They ate supper together and they talked about what would happen to them.

SIX

They nearly ran out of food on the plane because it was so crowded. It touched down at Dulles International shortly after three in the afternoon. Customs was easy because neither Ruth nor Kurt carried more than one suitcase filled with innocuous items of clothing. Passport Control was more dangerous.

The passports were very good, though, top quality, of the sort that only a man like Kurt Heinemann could obtain. The Federal Republic of Germany would have been proud to make its real passports as good as these counterfeits. Ruth Mesch and Kurt von Mannheim. Very good German visitors to the United States of America. Ruth stared around her like a Christmas morning child, beholding the wonders of the new world.

And then they were crossing the concourse to the taxi line outside and it was really done, finished, the long, difficult

37

escape from one life to another. Behind were rows of missing files pertaining to the Double Eagle and his network and to a lifetime of terrorism and espionage. Behind was the person of Ruth Sauer, once a betrayer of an American agent called November, now a schoolteacher on holiday in a country she had never known except as "that dreadful place."

The two men wore gray overcoats and hats. They smiled as they approached the German couple standing at the curb.

"My name is Winslow, Miss Mesch," the first man said. "And von Mannheim." Heavy on the "von Mannheim." The gray coats looked right through the girl into the eyes of the man. "We have nice adjoining rooms set up at the Willard and we would like to welcome you to the country."

Ruth turned her large, brown eyes to her brother. She bit her lip.

"No, no, *Liebchen*, don't be afraid," he said. But he was afraid. Was this a double-cross of everything he had set up?

"Not at all," Winslow said, answering the unasked question in Kurt Heinemann's black eyes. "We'd like to take you into the city, Miss Mesch, get you situated. Ah. Mr. von Mannheim, we'd like to . . . well, someone wants to meet with you and he didn't want to wait, so would you mind traveling separately?"

If this was some cross, then it was too elaborate, but one never knew. Americans got so caught up in planning things that they sometimes made them too complicated.

But what could he do?

"*Ja*, sure. Go ahead, Ruth, I'll meet you in the hotel. I will meet her in the hotel?" This to Winslow.

Winslow smiled like a toothpaste ad. "Sure, sure, there's nothing going on, just someone wants to meet you and couldn't wait. Okay?"

"*Ja, ja.*" But they were already taking her by the arm to the small gray government sedan and she looked back once at him fearfully and he had to smile for her. He gave her a little wave as well. The car pulled away with Ruth in the backseat. They stood on the curb and watched it pull away.

He turned to Winslow. "So?"

"So the big black Cadillac at the end of the taxi line," Winslow said without a trace of a smile now that it wasn't necessary. "Boss wants to see you."

Kurt Heinemann thought about it as he walked along the curb to the big car. Even if he had been crossed out of his deal, they had Ruth and this was their playing field and he would just have to stall along and look for an opportunity. That was the worst case. In the best case, they wanted to make friendly noises and maybe give him some money. He didn't really believe in either case just now; it was a way of preparing himself for the next bit of unexpected reality.

He entered the Cadillac's rear compartment separated from the front by thick glass. The car started up as soon as the door closed. The windows were shaded and the dull afternoon of clouds was rendered into early twilight.

Pendleton smiled at him. "*Wilkommen*. We meet again. Fifteen years. All things come to those who wait, even the fall of the Evil Empire."

"*Ja*. You told me once a long time ago to see you in Washington. You knew you were going to Washington some day," Kurt Heinemann said. Not the best case yet, not the worst. He sat rigidly on the gray fabric seat, eyes front.

"Not a doubt in my mind. Ran a brilliant desk in Europe for six years, got me a bunch of Russian spies thanks to you, went back into the headquarters and just worked my way up. Now I'm a successful man. You might say you helped make me. Except that wouldn't be polite."

"And what am I, Herr Pendleton?"

"You are a dirty fucking German spy with blood all over your lily-white hands is what you are, Herr Heinemann. You are on sufferance, is what you are," Pendleton said. The tone was pleasant, without any sense that the words were not.

"It can work that way," Kurt Heinemann said. He stared through the darkened glass at the darkened countryside. Suburban sprawl had long since overtaken Dulles, which had originally been built so far out in the Virginia countryside that no one ever expected the suburbs to catch it.

"Or it can work the other way," Pendleton said. "It's gonna take a few tricks but we are gonna put you in a nice place. Ever been to Denver?"

Kurt Heinemann shook his head.

He would not look at Pendleton because he wanted to hear the words from the brown-faced man and did not want to read any intent into them because of gestures made or eye contact. He was aware of Pendleton's eyes on him.

"I want you in Consortium International. You must have heard of it."

Kurt did not make any gesture.

"It's in Denver. Big contractor with a big budget but it is really all bullshit from beginning to end. CI is a CIA company. CIA don't own it but CIA is the reason it exists. It's a middleman for the CIA. It . . . does things for Langley. It acquires things for Langley."

"You want me to work for CIA," Kurt said. Flat, trying not to put anything in it.

"I beg your pardon, I don't think I said that at all. You, Kurt, are in the United Fucking States at my pleasure and my sufferance. You are working for me, Kurt, for Herr Pendleton. You are gonna work your skinny white ass off for me. I want you in CI because I want you to turn it. I want you to make CI bring home the bacon for Section, not Langley. I want you to work on what CI is working on, and when we get the goods, Langley will have to write off CI and CI will have to come to Section for its sugar. That's pretty clear, ain't it, Kurt? *Verstehen sie?*"

That turned his head. Kurt looked at Pendleton a long moment. A little anger in his eyes, a little rebellion. But not

40

now. Not this time. Not in this car. He looked away then, back to the side glass that artificially darkened the landscape.

"I did not expect this," Kurt said.

"No. And neither will Langley. It's a hard, cruel world and it is full of deceptions, ain't it? The world of spies is a shrinking world today, son. Langley, NSA, Section, DIA, the whole alphabet soup of agencies is being pushed around by the Commie lovers on the Hill who think the cold war is over and spies are history. Section never went into acquiring a sideline, like snooping industrial secrets. I want to expand into the business. Expand or die. You are gonna be my most secret agent, the one no one knows about except you and me. You are going to go into Consortium International and steal what they are now stealing for Langley and bring it to me. Like a good hunting dog." Pendleton was smiling, enjoying the humiliation of the German.

Kurt spoke in a soft, flat voice. "This is not right."

Pendleton just stared at him.

Kurt turned back to the man. "We agreed to a deal. I expect to give you information, tell you about Stasi. Not to be your agent."

"What you expect and what I expect are gonna end up being the same thing," Pendleton said.

"There are many, many like CI. Contractors. Middlemen." His tone softened. He was making a case to Pendleton. "You do not need me for this."

"Contractors you call them. They make a difference. CI is very big in the Pacific rim. They been buying up the territory. Spies. Agents. Industrial espionage. They do the dirty work and sell secrets to Langley. Last year, CI got hold of a new guided missile system for Langley that came out of China. Best thing the Chinese have made since they invented spaghetti. Consortium got the plans and even a model and sold it to Langley for thirty-four million dollars because they are a patriotic company. No one knows how they got it, no one says it was CI that got it, but there it is. I want that kind of power working for me. Working for Section."

"But I was Stasi. They won't—"

"Yes they will. You know all about something they want."

"What do they want?"

"You know about a Japanese machine. The mother of all code machines. Developing in a very secretive company in Japan. A machine that can read all the codes as well as make codes. The ultimate decoder."

"If you know this machine, get this machine yourself," Kurt said. But now he was interested. A moment before, he wanted to wrestle his way out of Pendleton's grip but Pendleton had him tight now.

"I can't. We don't know how to do that industrial voodoo. We'd screw it up. You get a piece of information from one station and a piece from someone with something to sell . . . Well, enough that I know this thing exists. And enough that you buy your way into CI by knowing it exists. The man at Consortium is named Gandolph. A greedy prick like they all are. You're gonna work for Gandolph because Gandolph wants the code machine. We should have it anyway; Japs been stealing our super silicones and building shit they don't have any right to in the first place. I don't know what Gandolph knows but I've prepared the way for you. Good reports on you. Resourcefulness. I been planting shit on Gandolph for months, waiting for you. Gandolph can get me the machine. He don't do dirty work. You do that for him. You get Gandolph the machine and then you force Gandolph to sell it to me and that dirties up CI in its relationship with Langley. I get a machine, I get Gandolph, I get CI and Langley don't get hind tit."

Kurt said nothing because he saw it, saw the parts of it.

Saw thirty-four million dollars as a real thing.

Saw a Japanese code machine that could be sold. To anyone.

Saw the beginning of a good solid double cross.

SEVEN

Pendleton had made the meeting short.

He had explained to Devereaux there was no disability.

Devereaux had stared at him without speaking for a long moment.

"Any deal you had with Hanley is over. Hanley ain't running Operations, I am. You and Hanley been acting like Section was your private piggy bank."

"The agreement was made," Devereaux finally said. He stared hard at the man behind Hanley's old desk and felt again the vague feelings of resentment he always felt when dealing with Pendleton. Going back to that meeting in Paris a long time ago.

The deal with Hanley was not in writing. These things never are. And Pendleton was tearing up the invisible paper this morning.

"I won't work for you," Devereaux said.

"What about all your years in service? What about duty and loyalty? What about your pension?" Light and mocking.

Devereaux got up.

"Siddown, November, I got things to say to you."

"I'm not November. I'm not in Section."

"Being in Section is like being a priest. It's a forever thing," Pendleton said. He frowned. "Siddown."

"Fuck you," Devereaux said.

Pendleton reached into the drawer to the right of the leghole under the desk. He pulled out a brown file. "Siddown," he said again and threw the file across the desk to the standing man.

Devereaux did not want to touch it.

He opened the file.

He saw a photograph and saw where this was leading.

He read the sheets.

There were other things as well.

He sat down to read them.

He threw the file on the desk.

"Rita Macklin," Pendleton said.

"None of that is true," Devereaux said.

"Truth ain't got nothing to do with it," Pendleton said.

And Devereaux was lost because it was pure blackmail and Pendleton had put it in pure terms. He could do this, he could destroy Rita Macklin even if it all turned out not to be true in the end. He would drag her through it and she would never recover from it.

And Devereaux saw that Pendleton would do just that.

"What do you want me to do?" he said finally.

Pendleton grinned. He couldn't help himself. "That's better. Welcome back on board. You were a good man once, now you prove yourself again."

Devereaux stared, tried to think through it. But there were only brick walls.

"Man in New York is very hard to get close to. I want you

to get close to him. Take your time. Leave your girl and get yourself a room in New York and advertise yourself. Ex-Agent for Hire. Intelligence for Sale. Something like that."

"Who is it?"

"Man named Mickey Connors. He's a middleman. Contractor. Works out of Hell's Kitchen. Does dirty things for Langley when Langley needs dirty things done. I want him in my camp. I want him to shovel shit for me when I ask him to do it. You're gonna get in and find out about him and you're gonna lead him to me."

"That's mole stuff. He wouldn't buy it. Besides, it'll take years."

"You got years, Devereaux. So's your girl friend. Nice career in D.C., girl reporter in the big time. I know this sounds crude, but life is crude. I'm trying to be as crude as possible so that you won't think for one minute I won't fuck you, fuck Rita, and fuck whoever else doesn't want to play the game."

"I might just take care of you," Devereaux said.

"There's always that possibility. But then, there's this file and it has a sister and how you gonna take care of that? Burgle R Section offices? Come on. Do what you're supposed to do and we'll get along all right."

He had walked home to Bethesda from Fourteenth Street. He had walked through the pestilential heat and seen nothing on the streets but his own thoughts. He was angry and drained at the same time. He thought of how he could kill Pendleton but that would be the easy part; the hard part was the files.

He walked across northwest Washington and was invisible to the city around him. He was pure thought but the thought was trapped by intangibles. He would end up doing what Pendleton wanted him to do because it was the only thing he could do.

Rita Macklin was the woman he loved.

They lived in their apartment off Old Georgetown Road in Bethesda.

It was a long walk on a long, steamy afternoon. He decided he needed every step of the walk.

He opened the door of their place and the air-conditioning chilled him suddenly and violently. He stood and shivered in the sudden cold and his shirt was wet and stained. The air rubbed a frigid hand on his chest. No, it was more than the air-conditioning. It was the sense of dread.

"Did you walk all the way back?" She stood in the kitchen, looking over the counter that opened on the living room. Her eyes were green and summer had brought out a ridge of freckles on her cheeks. She wore her red hair short now, all out of the style and fashion, because she was that sort of woman. The counter was littered with newspapers. She had been reading. Journalists are incurable.

"I walked back," he said, crossing to the bedroom. He didn't want to look at her. He still wasn't ready.

He took a long, hot shower and dressed in dry clothes. When he could not put it off anymore, he was still not ready to lie to her.

"What did they want?"

"A job."

"They can't—" She stopped herself. She saw it in his gray, troubled eyes. It was why he had walked home; he was wrestling with the bad things again.

"They can," he said. He crossed to the counter and still did not look at her. He took a bottle of Smirnoff and poured some in a glass and then opened the refrigerator and took out four cubes of ice. "I have to go up to New York in the morning."

"What's this about, Dev?"

"A job. A goddamned job." He slammed the drink down on the counter and she wanted to touch him. Instead, they looked at each other. Lovers, even when they lie to each other, tell the truth when they are just silent and just looking at each other.

"I love you, Rita, you know that." For a long time, he had not said those things to her because words were for lies. And then, by magic one day, he found a way to tell the truth. "But I've got to do this thing."

"They can't make you do it. You were put on permanent disability; they can't revoke it."

"They can do whatever they like," he said.

"You're not a slave. Didn't they ever hear of the Thirteenth Amendment?"

"Rita." He touched her. He held her. Lovers can more easily lie when they are holding each other. "It's a little job and it might take a few weeks but I have to be in New York most of the time. I'll try to see you if I can—"

"I can go to New York—"

"No."

Flat. Silence broke between them. They separated. He held her hand and then let it go.

They stood there and looked at each other.

"You can't tell me anything."

"I can't tell you anything," Devereaux said.

"Why can't they leave us alone?"

"I don't know. Maybe it's just Pendleton. He's the new broom at Section. He wants to shake everything up."

"Management technique. It'll pass."

"It'll pass," he said.

"But we have to take it in the meantime."

"In the meantime."

"What about New York? Aren't there rules about domestic spying?"

"There are lots of rules."

"I could write a story about you spying in New York. They wouldn't like that."

"They wouldn't like that," he said. He stared at her with grave eyes, eyes of infinite understanding. She was just angry now. He was angry. They might end up hurting each other if they stayed angry. He touched her again, slipping his hand around her waist. She was slim, with a runner's body. She let him draw her to him. She wanted to kiss him and did. Then she wanted to cry and did not.

"I can't bear it when you're not here," she said.

"I can call you."

"How long will it be?"

He said, "When I call you, Rita, we can't talk about the job. Not about being back on the job. We have to talk about being on permanent disability. You can't tell anyone I'm back in Section."

She shivered and it wasn't the air-conditioning. "You mean someone might be listening."

"It's very likely. In time."

"This is what they call going into black, isn't it? This isn't a little job at all, is it? Are you going to be . . . in danger? Don't do it, we can fight them—"

"We can't fight them."

"Dev, if you love me—"

"Don't even say that." He held her almost too tight. It took her breath away, the vise of his arms around her body. He held her tight the way a desperate man will cling to anything, anyone.

They made love on that last night. It wasn't very good between them though each wanted it to be. When lovers are going to separate, they can only think of the separation looming and they cannot take familiar pleasures in the same way. When lovers can believe they have all their lives ahead to making love, they can make love with selfishness and with satisfaction; but when time is short, they try to give too much to the other and they try to examine every act of instinct to impress it on memory.

He got up early, before dawn, and took down the bag in the hall closet and filled it with clothes. He didn't have a weapon and he had not asked for one. He zipped the little bag shut and rested it on the kitchen counter, on the pile of yesterday's newspapers. And she was there, in the archway that led to the bedroom. A single kitchen light illuminated the darkness of the apartment.

"You have to call me every night," she said.

"I can't do that," he said.

"Why?"

"Because we're separating," Devereaux said. It was the part he could not bear to tell her yesterday. "We are still friends, as they say in the gossip columns."

She didn't speak.

He looked at her. He had to remember how she looked now in her white satin nightgown and white robe, with her red hair disheveled. He had to remember the freckles on her breasts and the taste of her nipples and the feel of her thighs beneath his hand and the way she laughed when he licked her. He had to remember her.

"I'll call you in a couple of weeks." He cleared his throat. He looked away. "A couple of weeks." As though said to himself. "I'll call you when I can. I love you. Every night remember that. Nothing changed. I love you."

"But what can it be? How can they make you do this?" Her arms were folded across her chest and she stared at him hard now to see the truth.

"They can make me do this."

"What can it be? What hold can they have?"

"They can make me do this."

"Why won't you tell me? You can tell me."

"I can't."

49

"I'm losing you, Dev. I feel it. It's like bleeding. I'm losing you as we stand here."

"No. I'll never leave you."

"You're leaving me."

"I'll never leave you," he said. He wanted her to under-stand but the secret was in the way and lies were separating them. "I love you." He picked up the bag and walked to the door. He waited with his hand on the doorknob. Turned. She hadn't moved. "Always," he said.

He opened the door and left her.

EIGHT

14 Sept 90—NEW YORK CITY

He had a single room in an SRO hotel called the Croydon on the West Side. It was home to people starting out and people giving up, to dregs, drunks and ex-drunks, welfare recipients and people who were insane but who had been locked out of the insane asylum. He had one of the nicer rooms in the hotel because he paid and he looked like a man who would pay every week. His room had a private bathroom attached and a single Murphy bed. The sheets were changed once a week. There was a couch, an end table, a black-and-white television set, and, behind folding doors on one wall, a Pullman kitchenette. The hotel reeked with age and neglect and sadness. Nights were garish and loud on Tenth Avenue below the window; even when traffic finally died off, there were ambulances and fire engines in the neighborhood.

Devereaux explored this side of New York. It was full of

five- and six-story tenements hunkered low in the morning shadows cast by the high-rises going east from Seventh Avenue in the 50s. At the street level were delis and narrow newsstands and laundries and pawn shops. The neighborhood was littered with hard Irish bars, some of which did not seem to have any name.

Devereaux walked the streets. He felt his way into Hell's Kitchen the way he would have felt his way into the fabric of any foreign city. And he left a trail and wondered if anyone would notice it.

He thought of Pendleton most in the mornings, thought of a thousand ways to kill him. He thought of the sound of Pendleton's voice and swore he could hear it in the silence of his sleeping room.

And he thought of Rita Macklin all the time, at odd and painful moments. Once, he saw a redhead on Sixth Avenue and followed her for two blocks in the mistaken hope that Rita Macklin was in New York after all and was looking for him. It wasn't her.

He tried all the bars. The answer—or the beginning of one—was in these closed neighborhoods within the neighborhood. Dougherty's was on Eleventh Avenue. The bar was dark, the floor laid with broken white tile. There never seemed to be more than a half dozen souls in it, no matter the time of day or night. He would sit at the end stool in Dougherty's and drink beer from the single tap and watch television and not say a word to anyone.

It was the same in Grogan's on Tenth Avenue and McKee's—also on Tenth—and the Clare House on Ninth. Every place different and just the same. Every place lighted the same, day or night; every place containing silent, hard-faced men who sat at the bar and minded their own business, which was drinking.

But he kept going back to Dougherty's on Eleventh and he spent more time there.

Now and then, a man would come in and look at the barman and the barman would either shake his head or nod in the general direction of the washroom. When Devereaux used the washrooms, he saw a third door that led to a back room or office or storeroom and he decided this was where the men disappeared.

Sometimes a man would come into Dougherty's carrying a large display case like an oversized suitcase. He would look at the barman and the barman would nod almost imperceptibly and the man with the case would lug it into the back room and shut the door. And then, just as slyly, one of the denizens on the bar stools would slip off his perch and stroll toward the back as though going to use the washrooms. Except he would go into the back room as well. Devereaux thought it was very elaborate because they were simple thieves and fences and then he realized this was done because of his presence in the bar. He might have been a cop. In any case, he didn't appear to belong in the neighborhood; he didn't have the look.

It was frustrating, the endless, aimless days of waiting for something that he could not foresee. He did all the right things, went to the right places . . . and he waited. Worst, he could not call Rita, not in the first few weeks. It was part of the setup.

Also part of the setup was looking for work. He took an examination in French with a firm that serviced the UN with translators and interpreters. It was his best language; his Vietnamese was patois, a blend of French and native dialects that could get you understood in the jungle and not accepted in the velvet jungle on the East River. The firm said they'd get back to him; language facility was a commodity, after all, and some languages were worth more than others. There were a lot of French speakers; now, if he had spoken any Arabic . . .

He also tried a name remembered from his brief career as

a professor of Asian studies at Columbia University. He had been first recruited into R Section at Columbia. The name he had turned out to be dead.

He called Rita in the fourth week. He used a pay telephone in the dingy lobby of the Croydon Hotel. There was a telephone in his room but he wasn't going to make it easy on them. Whoever they would turn out to be.

It was late and she sounded drunk. She didn't drink very often at all and almost never to the point of slurring her words the way she did now.

"Are you all right?"

"Oh, shit," she said. "I'm fine. What about you?"

"Still looking for a job," he said. Waited.

"Looking for a job."

He waited. It was a little dangerous, he thought; she had been drinking and she might forget. And they might be listening. He waited still and he thought he could hear her breathing.

"Are you there?" she said.

"I thought I'd give you a call."

"I found some of your stuff. In the hall closet. When are you going to pick it up? Or you want me to dump it in the garbage?" Belligerent.

"I told you, I just wanted to leave it there—"

"Fuck you. You move out, you move out. Move out lock, stock, and barrel. I don't need your old suit hanging in my goddamned closet. My. Closet. My. Apartment. You get your ass down here and get your clothes."

He waited again.

"You there?" she said.

"Yes. I thought we could be friends."

"Okay, okay. So we're friends. Buddies. Bosom buddies. You liked my bosom, didn't you, buddy? You miss it? Well, I don't miss you. I want you to get your stuff out of my closet, buddy. Okay by you? Or I throw it out."

Silence on the line. He didn't know what to say.

"You gonna get your stuff?"

"I'll get it."

"When you gonna get it?"

"Soon."

"Give me soon. Give me a day so I don't have to be around."

"I'll come down Friday and get it," he said.

"Good. I got a date Friday."

"Rita," he said.

Nothing.

"Rita."

"See you, Dev," she said, and broke the connection.

He held the receiver in his hand for a moment and then replaced it on the hook. Then he hit the pay phone very hard with his fist and there was blood on his knuckles. He hit it again. The desk clerk, a fat young man with an earring, looked over at him. "Hey, don't take it out on the phone, buddy."

Devereaux thought he would like to push his fist into the pile of dough on the fat boy's face.

She had gutted him, just like that. His bowels were on the ground and more were falling out of his body and he couldn't hold them in. Just like that.

He went to Dougherty's that night but he wasn't looking for anyone, he wasn't dropping any names. He was staring at his own face in the mirror behind the bar exactly the way the other men stared at their faces, seeing the hopelessness in the eyes, letting the booze numb the aches that can't be reached by other medicines.

He saw Rita Macklin in his eyes. What had happened to her? But it was him. It was this stupid secrecy again, it was being back in harness again because a man forced him with simple, crude blackmail, the kind of blackmail that is usually most effective.

Devereaux drank until the bar closed at 2:00 A.M. and he had trouble walking home. It wasn't just the booze. It was the deep, dark hurt. Not only his but her hurt as well. The hurt in the voice on the phone, the angry kind of hurt that lacerates others but does most damage to the hurter.

He didn't even see the two men following him from the place.

Or the large black limousine the two men got into when he finally staggered up the steps of the Croydon Hotel and crossed the lobby.

The two men sat in the back of the limousine for a moment staring at each other. Then the young one, who was built big and had large, wide hands, looked at the older man and shrugged. It was his habit to shrug before he ever asked a question, as though to dismiss the question before it left his tongue.

"What do you think, Mick?"

"Ah, what I think is that it's a helluva performance if that's what it is, a helluva performance. We might be dealin' here with a real actor if that's all it is."

"If it is, we can know soon enough," Kevin said.

"That's the truth, lad. Soon enough. Mr. Devereaux's call to the stage has been made. Now let's see how deep the actin' can go."

"You think it's all an act then?"

"I don't know what I think." Silence. "But I do know how to find out, which is just as good."

NINE

15 Sept 90—NEW YORK CITY

Devereaux felt very bad all morning and into the afternoon. He tried to walk it out of his system. The walking helped but it made him think about her all the more. He tried to think of a way out of it but there didn't seem to be any. He had given it four weeks; could he go to Pendleton, cap in hand, and ask to be relieved, saying it had all failed? No, there was no possibility of that. And without that option, every other option collapsed.

The city was bright and warm; women in colorful dresses filled the sidewalks and some of them looked like Rita Macklin.

Night came in dark streets shadowed by tall buildings long before the sun set. He went back to the low-rise West Side of red brick tenements and Italian delis and Irish saloons. Give it another try. Devereaux walked to Dougherty's on Eleventh and climbed on the stool he usually used. The

57

nightman was skinny, with oily, curly hair worn long behind his ears.

"You wanna Harp?" His usual. He had come in enough times to have a usual drink.

"I want Scotch."

"We got no Scotch. Irish."

"Irish on the rocks."

The whiskey was smokey and harsh. No Scotch. Harp on tap. *Erin go bragh* behind the bar and a sign advertising a fundraiser for Northern Ireland Aid. Brits out. The hardness of the place had amused him at first and then it had begun to seep into his bones. It was too hard, harder than it had to be, but that was what the neighborhood was like. It was tough old New York with stickball, stickups, and a casual sense of life and death. He finished the drink sooner than he thought he had. He looked at the ice and then at the barman and nodded.

"Monday Night Football" was being played out on a color screen at the other end of the bar. The Giants were banging hard into the Bears and there were bodies all over the field. He stared at the screen—to stare at something—and thought he might just go back to Washington and wait until Pendleton called for his limousine and he would be the driver and he would take Pendleton out on Indian Head Highway down in Maryland south of Washington where there was a place to get rid of a body. He thought about that while he stared at the mayhem on the screen.

The man settled against the bar next to him. He had a long leather coat and it squeaked against the bar rail. Devereaux turned and looked at him. He was a small man with a face as pale as death. His eyes were very blue behind the wire-rimmed glasses. The line of his jaw and set of his teeth showed that he had seen everything in the world at least once. Devereaux had not expected this, not tonight, not this soon. He had already finished one whiskey and was halfway through another and he didn't feel ready for it.

"I like football. Reminds me of war. The way it really is fought, not the video games."

His voice was soft with the hard traces of an Irish accent in it. Devereaux turned to him. The barman had already poured a tall shot of whiskey for the man and left the bottle of Black Bush on the bar.

"That's why we like it, fella. You get the risk of death along with the game and you can bet on the whole thing besides. Snap a body, a tendon, break a back like Montana got his back broke a few years ago. That Stingley fella, paraplegic. That's war, a lot of broken bodies. God, they love it. Look at 'em." His contempt was as soft as his voice and it seemed to come so naturally, from such a deep place, that Devereaux could not say anything at all. The contempt was complete in itself.

"You don't look like a fella that likes football," the man said.

"I was out of the country when it got popular," Devereaux said.

The man smiled and raised his glass and drained it. A dash of color touched his pale cheeks. His hands were very large and he wore a wide golden band on the third finger of his right hand. His hair was thin and fine, spun with brown and gray threads.

"You been looking for me," he said.

"You're Mickey Connors," Devereaux said.

"The same."

"I been looking for you."

"You done all the right things. You stood out there and made your trail for me. You asked but you asked discreet. I like the way you did it. Even went up to the UN and tried to get a job. Jesus, I liked that. And looked up someone at

Columbia. You think you'd like to go back to teachin' after what you been doing the last twenty years?"

"I need a job."

"You gone down pretty far, ain't you, fella? Your girlie kicked you out, didn't she?"

"Nobody named you my father confessor."

Slow smile. Even smiling, there was an edge to him.

"You're a beautiful piece, Devereaux. I like all the little touches. You even call her from a pay phone because you figure I tapped the line. I did tap it. She sounded sloshed to me, does she drink heavy? I would guess she picked that up from you—"

"You would, huh? Go fuck yourself," Devereaux said.

Still smiling. "What are you, a tough guy? Lemme buy you a drink. Don't drink that shit he was giving you, drink this." And he poured from the Black Bush bottle on the rocks. "*Slanté.*" And they raised glasses and drank the whiskey.

"I just bought a drink for a drowning man," Mickey Connors said. He couldn't seem to get rid of the slow, contemptuous half smile that came naturally across his face.

Devereaux said nothing. The barman was down at the television set, watching Phil Simms set and throw. The same half dozen were at the bar, some staring at the dusty mirror and their own faces, some trying to focus on the game. The place smelled of bad beer pipes and spilled liquor. It was a party room that no one ever cleaned up after.

"You wanted me for something in particular?"

Devereaux judged the hard blue eyes. They were waiting for a lie. He couldn't do it, he knew he couldn't do it. It came up to this moment and he wasn't any good at it. He had known that from the start and it had sickened him all the more, thinking of Pendleton with that piece of blackmail paper on the desk between them, thinking he had to do his best and it wouldn't be good enough.

"I guess not," Devereaux said at last and turned away.

"Was it something I said?" Mocking still and just as softly delivered. He had been born in County Clare, Ireland, but he had come to New York at the age of five. Was the brogue just an affectation? But Devereaux had decided in that moment there wasn't an affected bone in Mickey Connors's body.

"I figure you stole enough in your time, you don't need a job," Mickey Connors said. "I know some things about you, Devereaux. Devereaux. Could be French or Irish, couldn't it? Or even English. What is it?"

"I'm from Chicago," Devereaux said.

The grin opened up. "That's a far country too, ain't it? But you ain't in Chicago now, fella, you're in Westie territory."

"What's this leading to?" Turned back to Mickey. Stared now. His eyes were as hard as the other man's but they were made of gray pewter, dulled by experience and the years.

"Come on, let's go for a ride."

Devereaux got off the barstool and scooped up his change. He noticed that no one in the place ever left a tip. And the barman never seemed to mind.

Eleventh Avenue was bright and dark at the same time. Orange lights cast orange shadows. The car was a stretch Cadillac sedan and the rear door was already open, held by a huge young man with wild black hair and black eyes.

They climbed inside and the big man slammed the door behind them and went to the driver's side. The glass between the front and back seats slid shut with a push of the button by Mickey's left hand.

Mickey Connors opened the bar and took out another bottle of Black Bush and two glasses. He poured and handed one to Devereaux.

"*Slanté*," he repeated the Irish language salute.

Devereaux did not say anything. He sipped the whiskey. The car was moving south in the light traffic toward the towers of lower Manhattan.

"Sit over there, I want to look you in the eye," Mickey Connors said. He nodded toward the jump seat. Devereaux shifted to the jump seat and stared across at Mickey. His arms rested on his knees.

"So what's the game, boy?"

"The same old game," Devereaux said.

"You in the trade or out?" Mickey Connors said, the half smile still teasing on his face.

"It depends," Devereaux said.

"The thing is, you dropped my name at a half dozen bars in the last month. You live like a fucking monk in that rathole room at the Croydon Hotel. I got interested in someone droppin' my name in my own block, so to speak. I checked around on you, all the way back. You was named November and you did a lot of shit in your time in Section."

"Did I?"

"Aw, come off it, fella, we're not doing 'Sesame Street' here. I see they gave you the dirty stick. Disability. You took out that fella in London was more than a year ago, name was Henry McGee, and they stuck you because of your accident. I even checked the accident. You were really hurt, no fake in that. I saw the X rays, how'd you like that? They was giving you LSD for a while there, didja know that?"

"The flashes were familiar."

"So they scrambled your brain and then they wiped you off the ledger." He shook his head. "The government is not a grateful employer."

He didn't have to lie for an answer. "They're assholes."

"I'll drink to that." He did. "I was involved in LSD, you know, in the early days when we were experimenting at Aberdeen Proving Ground in Maryland. Middle sixties. Couple of the volunteers decided to fly, some just went down the rabbit hole with Alice and never came back. One asshole did a Brody off the Flatiron Building. You figure you can fly, boy?"

"Only on United."

"So there's nothing wrong with you, is there? Except your girlie kicked you out and your life is taking a turn down the shit road?"

"We don't talk about her."

"Why didn't it work out? You were with her—"

"We don't talk about her."

"Well, I appreciate that. Leave the ladies out of it. Let's just say you were gettin' old and she noticed."

"The alternative to getting old isn't pleasant."

Mickey shook his head. "Death isn't so much, boy. It can be a positive release."

"I haven't swallowed so much philosophy since junior year at U.C."

"I ain't offering philosophy, boy."

"It doesn't look like you're offering anything except whiskey and a ride around the park."

"Oh, no. We're goin' someplace all right. Everything has a purpose."

"What's the purpose?"

Mickey ignored him. He stared out the window at the sullen streets and he might have been talking to himself. "Your clout in Section was this fella Hanley. He's the one kept you outta trouble. Now Hanley's been bumped and Pendleton is running Ops. Pendleton, that blue-eyed smoke bastard, I don't think he liked you."

"Maybe it was the other way around."

"It could have been. I can't get into Section very easy. I never dealt with them. But I know about that smoke. He's a mean bastard without a trace of humankind in him."

"You'd know about those things."

Mickey stared at him. "I know about those things."

Devereaux said nothing.

"You know where I come from? My old man and old man Kennedy was two corkscrews opening the same bottle of stolen wine, that's how far. My old man worked for him off the boat. I was five years old and I saw the way it was. Old man Kennedy liked to get Irish with me old man, sit down and have a few jars and talk about the old sod. Ah, fuck him. I saw the way it was. I did what my da dreamed of doing. He was never top man, couldn't get close."

"But you made it."

"I made it and I'm makin' it every day. I got a piece of a hundred coppers in Boston, New York, and Chicago. That's all you need, those three towns, good Irish lads every one of them and you can leverage all the rest. Those boys got eyes and ears. They can hear all the way into the heart of the G."

"What's the business, Mickey? Gunrunning for the IRA?"

"That too. That's my contribution, you might say. But you heard of me, don't be a shy fella now. You knew about someone named Mickey Connors when his name popped up in Nicaragua, didn't ya?"

"I might have."

"Y'see, Langley and me have a deal. I do for them unto others what they wouldn't be caught dead doing themselves. And they do unto me. If I can steal them a fur coat, I do it and they give me a pat on the back for it."

"You're an independent contractor."

"Among the big fellas. Like Consortium out in Denver. Like the Hairless Arab down in south Florida. The government needs us and we need the G. One dirty hand washing the other. You think what I do is bad compared to all the things you did in Section?"

"I don't think about Section. I'm thinking for myself."

"About time."

Silence. The big car swung into a narrow street that ran toward the docks on the Hudson.

"Where are we going?"

"You'll know when we get there," Mickey said.

"So everything has a purpose?"

"See, there was this copper. Copper from Chicago, in fact. Named Tubbo. One of my boys, he gets a regular check in the mail. Didja know a copper when you was little named Tubbo O'Neill?"

Devereaux stared at the man with the ghostly face.

"Tubbo O'Neill. I got connections and connections. He was part of my Northern Ireland connection. We get guns to the right people and Tubbo had his hand on my money in connection with doing my business. So the poor sap thought he'd steal some of my money, money for the cause."

Devereaux felt it then; it was like a chill. The words were runny and warm but they were hurtling along to someplace at a hundred miles an hour and Devereaux knew when they hit, it would be very bad.

"I caught him and made him pay up and put the juice on him. The vig goes on and on, that's the thing about it, you never can wriggle off it if I don't want you to. And I wanted to teach Tubbo a lesson and a lesson for any of the other boys who think stealing is for amateurs. I don't steal myself but I appreciate the pros."

"Is this going somewhere?"

Mickey Connors stared at him and for the first time, he let the smile fade. The car stopped. They were somewhere south of Hell's Kitchen in a neighborhood of darkened warehouses and meat lockers.

"It's going here," Mickey Connors said.

The big driver opened the door and Mickey Connors stepped out, the bottle of whiskey and the glass in his hand. He gestured with his head and Devereaux followed. They stood on the sidewalk. It was very dark here; the street's lights were out as though on purpose.

They crossed to a stairwell that led down to a steel basement door. The big man preceded them and opened the door.

They stepped into a boiler room. The lights were ablaze and there were three other men seated on packing boxes.

The fourth man must have been Tubbo. He was naked and hanging by his ankles from ropes tied to ceiling pipes. His white whale's belly was huge and flabby. His face was mottled red and he was breathing heavily.

Devereaux stepped into the circle of light. The other men looked up at him. They were making judgments, all of them. Devereaux stared at each of them. This was no time to look away. Finally, he stared at Tubbo.

"This fella is Devereaux. He made an inquiry or two into me and I been figuring out about him. He knows me and now I think I know him. He knows he might be useful to me and I think the same thing. But you never know, do you, boys?"

They didn't move or nod or make any gesture.

"Jesus, Mickey, for the love of God, lemme down," Tubbo cried. It was a strangled sound because the weight of his body was pressing on his diaphragm.

"In a little bit, Tubbo, just shush now," Mickey said. "I was saying, you gotta take the mark of a man. The way he handles whiskey or women. But I ain't in the business of women or whiskey." He looked at the bottle in his hand as though it startled him. He poured into the shot glass and drank it down. Again, color flashed briefly on his cheeks. He looked down at Tubbo's face and bulging eyes.

"Give him the piece, Kevin," Mickey Connors said. The big driver who had been standing next to Devereaux opened one giant hand and revealed a .38-caliber snubnose revolver. Devereaux took it in his hands.

"All right, fella."

Devereaux looked at Mickey. He nodded at Tubbo. Devereaux took a step forward and then looked again at Mickey Connors. The grin was back, lopsided on that deathly face.

Tubbo said, "Oh, my God."

Devereaux aimed at his chest and pulled the trigger. The shot exploded in the little room and Tubbo screamed. He pulled the trigger twice again.

There wasn't a mark on the screaming body.

He turned to Mickey Connors and no one had moved.

"Cut him down, Kevin," Mickey said.

Tubbo's body fell in a heap on the bare concrete floor. The three men on packing cases had not even flinched at the sounds of the shots.

"You can give Kevin the piece," Mickey Connors said in a calm voice.

Tubbo was sobbing on the floor.

"So what was the test about?" Devereaux said. His voice was flat, without any edge to it.

"About you and me, boy," Mickey said.

"No. I don't need it that bad. I don't kill people for a living."

"You were going to kill Tubbo."

"It was him or me, wasn't it, Mickey?" Devereaux said.

And Mickey Connors nodded now. "Exactly. It was indeed, lad. It was him or you. Except I wouldn't have used blanks on you, boyo."

"I guess I can walk back to the hotel now," Devereaux said. "I missed the end of the football game."

"Giants by ten," Kevin said. It was the first thing he had said.

Mickey Connors said, "Naw. We'll drive you back. You and Kevin run along; I gotta talk to Tubbo some."

"So what do I do next?" Devereaux said.

"Next? Next you meet me down at the Golden Dragon at noon. Place on Ninth."

"I know it."

"We'll eat some chink food and talk about next, fella."

And Devereaux could scarcely believe it. It had worked after all.

TEN

17 Sept 90—SANTA BARBARA, CALIFORNIA

Denisov had never gone California in his ten years of enforced exile. He wore a suit most of the time, even on hot days. He expected himself to wear a tie. He dressed in a conservative, dark way that would not have attracted any attention except in California.

The other man was Kurt Heinemann and there was something peculiarly European about him as well, though he wore tan trousers and an open-neck shirt. He was too lean and too muscular and he was untanned. His black eyes were too intense in the laidback culture and his gaze was too direct.

This was their third meeting. The meetings had been full of circles. Denisov understood that. People did not trust each other on first meeting in this trade.

That was why Kurt had sent Ruth to spy on Denisov from the beginning. She was reliable; she gave him all her

observations of the Russian living in Santa Barbara. What
Kurt could not have expected was that the urge came on her
again during her observation. It was not a disease in itself;
the doctor had once explained that. This nymphomania was
only a symptom of something else, something buried in her
subconscious that she could not face but tried to flee from
every now and then. That had been a long time ago in the
GDR. And now there was no GDR, only the Republic of
Germany united. Now there was nothing left at all of the
homeland except misery and poverty and angry crowds of
the unemployed and a collapse of order. It was hideous and
only his self-control was able to see a way for them out of
this, for Ruth and him, if only he could hold on a little
longer.

"Do you know that Ruth wants to live with me?"
Denisov said this carefully.

The other man stared out at the sea. They sat on a bench
at the edge of the beach. The beach was nearly empty because the day was so cool. There were oil derricks in the
water that marred the skyline. Santa Barbara stretched behind them up the steep hills to the mountains. Denisov
looked out to sea as well.

"*Ja.*" Silence. Ruth, Ruth. He shook his head. This was
such a complication in something that was complicated
enough to begin with. "Where is she now?"

"She went to Los Angeles today. She said she wanted to
buy things and to look at the city," Denisov said.

"So she already lives with you?"

"No. She lives in her own apartment. I did not expect this.
She is a beautiful woman, Kurt. I cannot refuse her. I am
. . . fond of her. She told me everything. She told me she
was to spy on me and that she could not do it."

"*Ja.* She falls in love." He made a face. "She has fallen in
love before, Herr Denisov. At times."

And Denisov blinked but did not look at the other man.

He had been a Soviet agent in KGB. He had even met Kurt once before, years ago, in Moscow. They were both exiles in this strange and wonderful country now and it was a bond of sadness between them, whatever business they had to transact.

"Would this be very serious?" Kurt Heinemann said.

"I am fond of her," Denisov said. "I was married. In the old country. I don't know what to say to you."

"It doesn't matter to me." He picked up a stone on the sand and flung it toward the sea. The stone splashed in the water.

"Ruth is my sister. She told you everything, no doubt. She told you about our family history. So, you have the advantage to me. I only met you one time in Moscow a long time ago. So. You have something that I am willing to pay you for and that is that. What it is for Ruth is for Ruth to decide."

"I think it might be better not to deal with you now. In this matter. This is too . . . personal now."

"*Ja*. Too personal." They both saw it, both saw Ruth flitting across their interior visions. It was a stupid complication the way most complications are.

"So I will make another arrangement." The Russian wore rimless glasses and his mild blue eyes might have belonged to a saint in another age when there were still saints in the world. He was large and gentle in his movements unless he had to act in violence. And then he could still move with cruel certainty.

"I want that machine," Kurt Heinemann said. His voice was very quiet.

"But I cannot trust you now," Denisov said. "You are too . . . close."

"*Ja*. Too close. So you trust me less than you trusted me a month ago, huh? I am in a difficult position, Herr Denisov. You can get something I want. I can pay you, which is something you want. But you and I . . . well, she is a girl and it doesn't matter to me. I want to survive and this is part of my survival. I shouldn't have used her but I trust her, the only person I trust to see the way clear for me. So I make you a bargain, Herr Denisov. I will take her away and lock her up for you so that you can trust me again."

"No."

Said too softly, too quickly.

Kurt stared at sea gulls circling.

"I live alone," Denisov said.

"*Ja, ja.* We all live alone, even when we're married. But you have some money, eh? A man with money chooses to live alone."

"She is young. She can make me laugh."

"She is a silly woman," Kurt said. "You should not grow too fond of her."

"When will you have the money?"

The change was so abrupt that Kurt nearly missed it. Speaking in English all the time was wearying; there was too much thought connected with it. He had been lost in thinking about Ruth, about how to sever this complication. He sometimes thought he might kill Ruth, just to finish the matter and put her at rest with herself. He might have been thinking about that now when Denisov changed the subject.

"The money is no problem. The problem is your package."

"It's very close now."

Kurt glanced at him. But Denisov was looking out to sea.

"How close is it?"

"Close. A matter of weeks. Not many weeks. And when it comes, it must be done quickly so we can sweep up the trail. There will be people looking for that package."

"The Japanese."

"*Da.* Japanese, and there are others. The business is growing. You know that. Industrial designs. Secret patents. Papers. Plans. All the software and the hardware that follows."

"We are talking about the plans for this computer?"

Denisov shook his head. "That cannot be done. It is easier to steal the finished product."

"Where is it?"

"Still in Hokkaido, locked inside Masatata Heavy Industries. The security is very good. They have contracted with one of the largest gangs in Japan for security. Everyone is very jealous of the machine they are building."

"Is it built?"

"I think so," Denisov said. "Yes. I think it's ready to be moved. That is my best thinking. It is ready to be moved."

"To where?"

"Tokyo. The Japanese government wants to look at it and test it."

"What kind of a code machine is it?"

"A computer. But it's not a code machine, my friend. It is something more. I think it is much more now. I too thought it was a code machine."

"What more?"

Denisov shook his head.

"I want one million dollars a week from today. That is for my necessary . . . arrangements."

"That's a lot of—"

Denisov waved his hand. "Stop. Don't argue with me. I set the price on everything. The machine will cost you fifteen million dollars delivered. And one million beforehand for expenses and as a gesture of your faith."

"Why would I trust to give you one million?"

Denisov looked at him with his mild eyes. "Because you do not trust me and I do not trust you. At some point, we must stop this circling around and around." He gestured circles with his index finger. "I am not doing this for my exercise. I have a machine that you will pay fifteen million for. And one million in expense."

"You don't have anything at all. You said so."

"But you have your spy on me," Denisov said. "She watched me and watched me and whatever she could tell you, she's told you. Four months. She sees me when I leave in the morning. She knows the license plates of people I meet. She knows the women I took home with me. You know everything she told you and yet you know nothing."

It was completely, utterly true. Every thread was examined and, in the end, Denisov appeared to be nothing but a retired gentleman living in Santa Barbara with a small clique of acquaintances, who played chess once a week with another Russian crony, and who gambled on the stock market. Nothing at all. It was either true—Denisov was nothing and he wanted to con Kurt Heinemann's company—or he was a clever spy and illegal trader in other people's secrets. Consortium knew about Denisov from Kurt Heinemann; it was why they had accepted him as an operator, at least on a trial basis after examining his bona fides from the Stasi files and other sources in the illegal trade.

Sources planted by Pendleton.

And Pendleton said Denisov was in the trade and he would come up with a code machine that could be used to turn Consortium International into a supplier for R Section.

"I will try," Kurt began.

"No. I do not expect a good effort. Just a good result."

"You know how these things work."

Denisov gave him a sharp look then. "*Da*, Herr Heinemann. I know how things work. And so do you. We are at the point where they say to cut your bait."

Silence for a long moment. Then Heinemann nodded just once.

"All right."

The two men rose as if on signal and started away from the bench going in opposite directions. Heinemann stopped after a few paces and looked back. Denisov was walking away without concern, an absurd dumpy man in a dark gray suit and white shirt and tie on a California beachfront. Kurt almost felt kindness toward him in that moment; what were they both but tools for others, set up in exile in a country of exiles?

The feeling of kinship passed.

He would kill Denisov in the end, of course. And take the machine and the money back to Germany. The one big Germany but still the Germany where there were many Stasi exiles wandering around, wondering what had happened to them and the state they had served. Fifteen million dollars for a new beginning for a new network of people who could be trusted to think the same things. It was a lot of money. And the machine. He had given that a lot of thought as well. All governments were the same, even the government at Bonn. Perhaps they could find a place, gratefully, for both the machine and the spy who brought it to them.

ELEVEN

This time Devereaux walked into Dougherty's at 10:00 A.M. and the day bartender nodded at him and pointed toward the back room.

Devereaux pushed open the door. Mickey Connors sat alone at a small desk with a business checkbook in front of him. He was peering at a sheet of paper. He put the paper down and looked up and tried a small smile. Devereaux sat down in the hard wooden chair across the desk from him.

"The trouble with this business is everyone gets the attitude that stealing is all right to do," Mickey Connors said. He shook his head. "They steal a little and I let 'em and then, every now and then, they start to steal too much."

"You should deal with a better class of people."

"There ain't no better class. Everyone's a thief when it comes down to it."

"Who's stealing?"

"Ah, just the boys running the bar. I'll have a word with them. Or maybe I'll let Kevin have a word with them. You gotta exercise a young fella like Kevin, like a good racehorse, let him feel his oats now and then."

Devereaux waited. It was Thursday and he had met twice with Mickey Connors and had no idea where any of this was going. Maybe Pendleton had no idea either but he doubted that.

"All right. Now our business." He took off his glasses and laid them on the desk.

"What is our business?"

"You put away a Soviet agent ten years ago. His name was Denisov. Does it ring a bell?"

"Why should it?"

"Because he's trying to get in the trade and I think the field is too crowded the way it is now. He's out in California where your Section stashed him ten years ago. For the last six months, the trade is talking about something coming out of Japan that we want. We all want."

"What do we want?"

"Nobody knows exactly. But this big Jap outfit called Masatata Heavy Industries is developing something. The thing is, it's a secret but it has to do with cryptography. They're making some kind of code machine. The Japs been getting our superconductor chips even though the American companies that make them been told not to sell them abroad. You see the way of it, boy? The world is full of thieves and nobody obeys the rules." He shook his head at the perfidy of mankind.

Then smiled in a slow, secret way. "Langley has heard about it but they've got no contact with this fella Denisov. He was Section property, same as you, because you turned him."

"That was a long time ago."

"Langley hears things. Out of Hawaii, of all places. This

fellow Denisov from Santa Barbara, California, keeps coming over to talk shipping business. Only he talks to the wrong people. A fella named Peterson runs dope into the islands on his boat and that's the kind of low-life this buyer from Santa Barbara is talking to."

"Denisov."

"The very same fella. Interesting, ain't it? You just happen to turn up at a time I could use a fella like you. And you knowing the territory and all."

Devereaux waited. There was always an edge in this playful manner, he had learned that much about Mickey Connors.

"Well, that's all Langley could tell me. They hear about the Japanese code machine same as everyone else but nobody even knows if the damned thing exists. Except this fella Denisov, he knows it exists."

"Why?"

"Maybe I got a fella in Consortium International. Maybe I got a spy and maybe the spy tells me that they been trying to work out a deal with some fella for something that is Japanese and smaller than a breadbox. You follow me?"

"I'm trying."

"I've got a good set of ears inside Consortium. You might say we're sort of business rivals in a small world. We both deal with Langley—but you know that, don't you?"

Devereaux said nothing.

Mickey scratched his ear and stared at the other man for a long moment.

"I want to know what you want, Devereaux," Mickey Connors said.

"Maybe we want the same things."

"Anything's possible."

Devereaux decided to advance it a square at a time. "Consortium is going after the Japanese machine, whatever it is. A decoding machine, the mother of all decoding machines.

This country would build one in . . . what do they estimate?"
He looked at Mickey.

Mickey smiled. "Ten years. Japs are ten years up on us. We'd sure the hell like to have a look at a finished code machine."

"So it would be worth money to someone."

"Ah, stop dancing me, fella. Whoever steals the machine is sitting on a small fortune."

"But first, the thief has to deal with the first thief. Denisov. In Santa Barbara. Denisov gets the decoder machine and gets his payoff. And the middle man middles it back to . . . who do you think wants to pay top price for it, Mickey?"

"It ain't the fuckin' Russians for sure," Mickey Connors said.

"Langley," Devereaux said.

"So it's always been."

Silence.

"Do you think there might come along another bidder?" Mickey asked. He was staring at his manicured fingernails. They needed a trim.

Devereaux watched the other man's hands as well. He decided not to answer.

"In any case, that's down the line." Mickey looked up. "I want to use you, Devereaux, you've got a cool eye and I know a little about you. You've stepped out of the traces from time to time. Maybe you can do me a favor."

"Get the machine when Denisov gets it."

"Naw, naw, I'm not a fool. I don't exactly trust you but I can see some angles. Maybe you want the machine for R Section. Maybe you want to cut me out. Or maybe you want me to sell it to R Section. Or maybe you're really on the beach and you want a new start in life. And maybe that blue-eyed smoke you work for—"

Devereaux held up a hand.

"—All right, did work for once and maybe work for still,

maybe he can be a man to deal with. I don't know and that's the truth. But if I cut you out now, I'll never find out, will I?"

Devereaux said, "Probably not."

"I don't want you going against Denisov. You and Denisov go back, don't you? A couple of peas in the old cold war days."

Devereaux tried not to look surprised.

"I know you, lad, I know about you. You got sufferance due you because I don't know enough. You want a job from me? Then you go out to California and you watch. I want to know who Denisov is dealing with from Consortium. I can't get it from my ears and I think time is running down."

"Your spy inside Consortium must not be very good," Devereaux said. Said it as an aside, as though it meant nothing.

"Consortium is a funny place. A bunch of boxes lined up with locks on them. One box never knows what goes on inside another box. I want to get a line—quick—on who is dealing with Denisov. And I want to leave Denisov in place. When he gets the code machine, the outfit he steals it from is gonna come after him hard. Let Denisov take a fall. When I get the machine, I'll figure out who the highest bidder is gonna be. You fellas at Section or Langley."

"Maybe I'd get the machine ahead of you."

Mickey stared at him. "I want you out there, Devereaux, because it's safer than if you was off sneaking around. You contact me through Dougherty's bar. You watch Denisov and you find out who the middle man is he's dealing with. There's a Mr. Inside on this and a Mr. Outside. I know who's inside."

"Who?"

"That's for me to know. A man of long standing in CI. But he's gotta have someone working for him, making the contacts with Denisov. That's what you find out, fella, and you'll have done me a favor."

"What's that mean for me?"

"Terms. Two thousand a week for now. And it means you did Mickey Connors a favor."

Devereaux smiled then. "But I might end up with the decoder machine. You're taking a risk."

"It's all about risks." Mickey stood up. "I take risks, you take them. But it's all worth it for the game. And for the money."

"Don't forget the money," Devereaux said.

And Mickey Connors gave him a glacial look that turned blue eyes into ice fields.

"And don't you forget Tubbo there, hanging upside down. Naw. You wouldn't wanna forget that at all, fella."

TWELVE

18 Sep 90—DENVER

Consortium International. The *CI* of the powerful logo had been designed by a firm that did such things. It featured a stylized globe embrace by the *C* and slashed across with the *I*. The logo was rendered in brass in the lobby and again in smaller brass on the mahogany door to the suites on the twelfth floor.

Denver was bright and pretty in the afternoon sun and office workers held picnics on benches along the Sixteenth Street mall. There were streaks of snow in the higher elevations of the Front Range, which formed the perfect backdrop to the glittering cityscape.

Gandolph had called him in for a 2:00 P.M. appointment. Kurt Heinemann felt uncomfortable in the offices of CI the few times he had been there. He did not know these people; therefore, he did not trust them.

He always presented himself to the secretary as a stranger.

Mr. Henry Dodge. All his dealings with CI were through Gandolph, the CEO.

She led him into an empty office and assured him that Mr. Gandolph would be there shortly. It was always the same with Gandolph; he made entrances, usually five minutes behind schedule. It annoyed everyone and was meant to do so.

Kurt did not sit down. He crossed to the window wall and looked down at the sunny street full of office workers enjoying the sunshine. He saw everything and thought nothing of it; his thoughts were all interior, formed by Ruth and Denisov and by the job at hand. It was a way to get through it all, to never look around or deviate from the path chosen.

"Mr. Dodge."

He turned and Gandolph stood at the doorway smiling. Gandolph always smiled. He wore a rep tie and light blue oxford cloth shirt and ran thirty miles every week. Kurt thought he didn't have any flab on his body and yet it looked soft anyway. His resentments—of fleeing the GDR, of working for Pendleton—focused themselves now on Gandolph.

Gandolph closed the door and turned on the noise machine. The offices were all swept for bugs at least weekly but the noise machines were part of the security.

"How are you?"

"He says it is close, within weeks. He wants one million dollars for operations delivered in five days."

"Nice day, isn't it?" Gandolph's smile was strained.

Kurt Heinemann waited. He hated pleasantries.

Gandolph went around the desk to the credenza and poured himself a cup of decaffeinated coffee. He didn't bother to offer Kurt a cup.

"That's a lot of money, Kurt."

"Come on. You knew what this would cost in the beginning."

"And you still trust your . . . contact." Gandolph did not know Denisov, not even his location.

"The customer is satisfactory. I think he will try tricks but I know all the tricks."

"I bet you do, Kurt."

"One million."

"You can pick up the money tomorrow."

"I think not. I don't want to come to this place twice in the same week. I want to be anonymous."

"I appreciate your caution. Even more this morning."

Kurt Heinemann picked up the change in tone. He studied Gandolph's face. He did not want surprises and he thought a surprise was coming.

"We have a little problem. A very little problem. At least, I think it's a little problem," Gandolph said. He was smiling absently like an idiot or a daydreamer. He reached in the pocket of his sports jacket and took out a piece of paper.

"We've been running a security check. On some of the new employees, less than a year. Routine. We get records from the telephone company on their home calls."

"Who?" he said.

"My secretary," Gandolph said. "Miss Browning. She let you into my office. Actually, she's worked for me less than a month but she worked in operations prior to that. We hired her last November."

"And she made calls."

"Yes. Three calls last month. To New York. She's from Arizona originally. Family there."

"Who did she call?"

"We don't know."

Kurt stood very stiff and still and tried to blot out the image of this grinning idiot and to keep the image formed by the words. He saw Miss Browning in his mind: Brown suit, white blouse, low brown heels, blond hair, light brown eyes. Yes.

"They were all placed to a bar of some sort on Eleventh Avenue in New York. The barman answered each time. It's called Dougherty's. We called in six times and that was all we got, some voice saying, 'Dougherty's.' "

"What is that place?"

"There's a man named Mickey Connors who runs an organization that doesn't even have a name. No offices. An untraceable man of many parts who would love to do harm to Consortium. We're . . . business rivals, you might say."

"I never heard of him."

"You would in time. He started in business as an arms dealer. He doesn't make things, he sells things. Things and services. A traveling salesman. He's never been much bother to us because he never had the patience to go after hardware. Stuff like the stuff we're dealing for with your contact. You understand?"

"I understand."

"The problem is, we think she is a spy for Mr. Connors."

"What are you going to do?"

"Fire her."

"And she will go to New York then and tell this Connors man everyone you meet with? Describe them, give them names? Give them my name?"

"Mr. Dodge."

"*Ja, ja,* Mr. Dodge, who is six feet tall with a white scar on his face and who has black eyes and weighs about one hundred sixty-five pounds. Mr. Dodge with a valid German passport who entered the country less than a year ago. And where did Mr. Dodge who is Mr. von Mannheim really come from? Good, Mr. Gandolph, that is a very good idea."

"You don't have to use that tone."

"I have to because you keep smiling like this is a joke."

"It is no joke. I'm a pleasant person and I smile a lot."

"And Miss Browning. Does she smile a lot too?"

That stopped the smile.

Silence save for the gurgle of the noise machine.

"Well, then. What should I do in this case? Allow her to continue her espionage?"

"I think you should give Miss Browning a package tomorrow morning and ask her to deliver it. To Mr. Dodge. That is what I think."

"And then what?"

"And then nothing."

Silence again. Gandolph fingered his tie in a characteristic gesture.

"Any . . . untoward act would trace back to Consortium. She works here. We sign her checks."

"*Ja, ja.* But she had turned in her notice two weeks ago, isn't that right? Isn't that what you do in this country when you take another job?"

A nervous tic replaced the smile. The tic started at the corner of Gandolph's right eye. Kurt stared at him the way he might stare at a television screen. He thought then that Gandolph would have to be involved and it was a good way to start it. With Miss Browning's disappearance and Gandolph's lies to cover her disappearance. For the first time, Kurt saw his way clear, saw exactly what he would do to cover all his trails when the time came, to win both the fifteen million dollars and the Japanese code machine and—more important—to get away with it.

"All right. Just nothing to lead to us?"

"No. Does she live alone?"

"In an apartment out south."

"*Ja.* Okay." Wearily. Another complication. "I want you to have Miss Browning deliver the money in the morning. To the house on Eighteenth."

"And then what?"

"Then . . . nothing."

"I don't want to be involved with murder."

It was incredible. What did he think this was all about? The details of murder and terror were never spoken of in polite society. That was garbage work left to someone like Kurt Heinemann to take care of. Kurt could not help it; cold contempt froze his features for a moment and even Gandolph saw it.

"You won't be involved. It won't even be murder if it is done correctly. Just have her go to the house on Eighteenth Street in the morning at eleven."

"All right." Gandolph looked away from the hard German face and black eyes. He walked to the window wall and looked down at the sun-worshipers.

"There is something else," he began.

Another surprise.

"Fifteen million dollars," Gandolph said.

"It was the price from the beginning. He wouldn't haggle it down. He said it was worth more than that. To us and to whomever we sold it to."

"We only have one government customer who would pay for it," Gandolph said. "Maybe we couldn't get the price."

"You have more than one customer in any case," Kurt said. "Sell it back to Masatata Heavy Industries if you want."

"You mean the Japanese would buy it back?"

"Why not?"

"They'd . . . lose face."

"Face? The Japanese lost face when they lost the war. They have the honor of thieves. They pretend to honor but it is pretense, Herr Gandolph. They would grovel, *ja*. They would pay just like that."

Gandolph smiled then. The tic disappeared. "I suppose you would know about that. The Germans, I mean."

Kurt Heinemann felt the insult but it was a pathetic thing, like a child's slap. "*Ja*, some Germans lost their honor and traded it for television sets and Mercedes sedans and full bellies, just like the Americans. But there are still Germans, Herr Gandolph, you can believe that. And the Japanese code machine will have many buyers, you can believe that. My . . . contact . . . is not impatient. If we don't deal with him, he can find another to deal with. Maybe this Irish man in New York who put a spy on your staff."

Gandolph flushed. "Mickey Connors never got into anything this big."

"Perhaps he is . . . expanding."

The flush stayed on Gandolph's face and deepened.

"You see, Herr Gandolph?"

"I also see this fifteen million, Mr. Heinemann. Fifteen million is real money, not toy money. What if your . . . seller . . . could be persuaded—in some way—to relinquish the machine and give back the fifteen million dollars?"

Ja. Kurt smiled at that. "Everything is possible but he isn't a stupid man. He has a Swiss account. He wishes you to deposit the money in the Swiss account at the time of his choosing, when the code machine is turned over."

"Zurich accounts can be . . . breached. We've done that before."

"Is that possible?"

"Oh, yes." The superior smile returned. "Everything isn't rough and ready in this business. There are subtle aspects."

Ja, ja. Kurt managed to look puzzled while trying to block another siege of contempt overcoming him. Who did Gandolph think he was, a baby? A simple wet contractor? When the time came, it would be Kurt Heinemann with the fifteen million as well as the code machine, the wonderful code machine that would change the very nature of cryptography. Who wouldn't want the machine? And with all the money from selling it combined with the money he would steal from Denisov, Kurt Heinemann would be very able to go back into business, this time not for the Russians but for his own German network.

"Then let us see when the time comes," Kurt Heinemann said. "You will tell me what to do when the time comes."

Kurt saw that Gandolph liked this. The bureaucrat instructing the garbageman, the contractor giving out his wet contracts and thinking he somehow shared the danger of them in that moment. *Ja, ja,* Herr Gandolph, and let me doff my hat to you.

"Well . . ." Gandolph looked around him. "I suppose we shall have to wait on your . . . client. And not very long, eh?"

"Not too long," Kurt said.

"All right. Then I'll send along . . . the money tomorrow morning. By special courier." He smiled, pleased at his euphemism. It sounded very inside, very much in espionage.

"As you say," Kurt said. He was being dismissed. He inclined his head once, quickly, a gesture of assent. He went to the door and opened it. Miss Browning was behind her desk. Eyes gray, not brown, he had not been as observant as he thought. Miss Browning smiled at him. "Mr. Dodge," she said. The smile was very bright and Kurt returned it.

Gray eyes, not brown, he thought, leaving the outer office and entering the hall.

THIRTEEN

20 Sep 90—WASHINGTON, D.C.

Devereaux bought a ticket on a Delta flight bound for Los Angeles that had to go through its Atlanta hub. He had planned on Mickey Connors having one of his watchers trailing him at LaGuardia but he figured even Mickey Connors didn't have anyone in Atlanta. He also bought a nonstop ticket on American from New York to Los Angeles. The planes left within twenty minutes of each other. Did Mickey Connors have an in with the airlines? Could he check tickets? Devereaux wasn't sure. But he was sure that Mickey Connors was setting him up, either because of his own inherent caution or because he suspected the truth about Devereaux.

In any case, he had to see Rita Macklin.

The flight to Atlanta was bumpy but boring. Twice Devereaux strolled from his first-class seat to the toilet at the back of the 727. Each time, he searched the faces in all the seats.

What was he looking for? He was just watching his trail and he wasn't sure he had the skill to pick out anyone who might be watching him.

Hartsfield International is a long nightmare of plastic that endlessly replicates itself throughout the terminals. So many feet between identical bars, identical restaurants, identical newsstands; there is no sense of a beginning or ending to these airport shops or, indeed, any sense of being anywhere in particular in the world.

Devereaux caught a Delta flight to Washington National. The taxi ride from Washington to Bethesda took forty minutes.

Had he misread her slurred message that night? She was throwing him out and told him to pick up his clothes on Friday or they would be tossed in the garbage. Perhaps it was true. Perhaps they had both understood that the line might be tapped, by either Section or someone else. Like Mickey Connors.

Was he putting her in harm's way?

He stood on the front stoop of the building and waited while the cab pulled away. He waited for ten minutes. The street was empty in the bright late morning light and there was no traffic at all in those ten minutes. The apartment had suited them; it was quiet and anonymous and the perfect hiding place for lovers who have no need of any amenities except themselves.

He opened the apartment door with a key. She was sitting at the kitchen counter on a stool, typing into a laptop Zenith word processor. She looked up as he entered and he understood.

He kissed her very hard and she began to cry and shake and he held her for a long time until she could stop crying and stop shaking.

"I thought maybe I got it wrong," he said.

"Oh, Dev. I was so angry with you all those weeks. You

never called and I couldn't reach you and I thought even if you were killed, they wouldn't tell me. I got angrier and angrier. And then, three days before you called, I went to see him."

He held her apart to better see her eyes. They were red with tears but there was something else; they were eyes that had seen too much too soon.

He didn't ask who.

"Oh, hold me again."

He held her and she buried her face in his chest. He thought she might break in that moment but there were no more tears. When she stepped back from him, he could only gaze at her and wait.

She went into the kitchen and opened the refrigerator. She took out a carton of 2 percent milk and poured it into a glass. She drank the milk and put the glass down on the counter. She looked at the glass of milk and began to speak in a slow, uninflected way that was curiously outside her, as though another person were making a report.

"I went to see Hanley at first but he transferred me to this man who had replaced him. He wouldn't even see me. Just a security guard who took me to this other man. His name is Pendleton."

Devereaux waited. Silence ticked like a clock between them.

"Pendleton said you were doing a mission. He called it that. A mission. He seemed amused by me. He said he had no idea where you were or what you were doing. He said it was a secret."

"He told you the truth."

"I didn't believe him at first. He wanted to know if I had spoken to you on the phone. I said he ought to know, he probably had my phone tapped. He laughed at that and then he said, 'The tap doesn't belong to us.' He said it without any indication of what it meant. I figured he had checked the telephone for a tap and discovered it and left it in place. That pissed me off along with everything else."

"So you knew it was tapped."

"I guessed it was. I guessed that part of what you had to do was to make them, whoever they are, believe you and I were separated."

"Yes," Devereaux said. "I told you I loved you."

"Damnit, why didn't you tell me."

"I don't want you to get involved in this. I don't even know how it's going to end up—"

"Why did you do this for that man, Pendleton? I really hated him after ten minutes. Another ten minutes and I could have gotten a gun and shot him."

"He has that effect on people," Devereaux said.

"Why are you working for him?"

"Because I have to."

"Damn you, damn you. This filthy trade always comes between us."

It was true. He couldn't defend it. Or himself.

"Oh, honey." Spoken with a voice on the edge of despair. "Dev, whatever it is, you have to tell me. You have to share it with me. We have to share some things."

"No," he said. "You've got a real life. You write about news, real people, real things. I've got lies and secrets and deals you don't ever want to know about."

"So how long will this go on?"

"I don't know. I have to satisfy someone's idea of when the job is finished. I don't know; Pendleton knows."

"If you hadn't shown up today, I would have gone to New York and found you. I really would have. I know someone on the *Times*. I would have told her the story about you and they would have put your picture in the paper and—"

"And then I would have been dead. And the problem wouldn't have been resolved." Devereaux turned from her and went to the picture window that looked down on the brilliant autumn woods behind the building. There were traces of red and yellow in the still luxurious green on the trees.

"That's your instinct, Rita. You're a reporter and you tell things. That's why I can't tell you my things. It isn't a matter of trust. I love you and I trust you. But you don't need these secrets and you don't need to know the bad things. All the bad things."

"So you won't tell me."

"I can't."

Silence. They sat down across the counter from each other and let the silence feed on itself. She went to the refrigerator freezer and took out a tray of ice and prepared two glasses. She poured Red Label scotch in them and gave him one.

"I was in a bar so Irish that they wouldn't serve you Scotch," Devereaux said. It made him smile now; it was a world removed from her. Maybe that was it. If he told her everything and shared the secrets, it would hurt them both, hurt the thing they had together.

"Where was it?"

"On the West Side. Manhattan. A different kind of New York."

"What was it called?"

He glanced up then. "I don't remember."

"You're lying again. You can't even tell me that."

"It was Grogan's or something. I just forgot it."

"You never forget," she said.

He tasted the Scotch. The Irish whiskey had been drunk that night to ease the pain of her anger and her words. He hadn't figured out her coded message to him—if it had been a coded message and if he wasn't just reading it into her words to give himself a bit of hope—until the next day when Mickey Connors had introduced him into his world. He tasted the Scotch now and thought about the nature of his world of lies.

"Pendleton wants me to infiltrate an organization run by an Irish fellow named Mickey Connors," he said, staring at the drink in his hand. "Mr. Connors is one of the world's middlemen in the trade. He does dirty work for the CIA and he sells illegal arms and he can manage to get things for Langley that more straightforward organizations can't get. He works in the dark side of a dark business."

"Like the old Mafia connection with the CIA."

"Like that. Giancana and those people trying to knock off Castro in the sixties. Like the Arab in Florida who sells arms to people in the Middle East. Sometimes they're useful."

"What does Pendleton want exactly?"

"I'm not sure but I'm beginning to understand. There's something out there that a lot of people want. I guess it's some kind of code machine, only better and faster than any machine before. Do you know what a one-time pad is?"

"No."

"It's a way of sending secret codes. You use a sequence of numbers that are contained in a book that's the key to the code. The sender has the key and the receiver has the key. You use the code once and even if it's overheard, it can't be broken because there's not enough in the message to piece together the sequence. You know, so many Es in a code or As or Ms."

"All right."

"But one-time pads can be broken by the weight of the information that has to be transmitted. Cipher clerks are like everyone else, they cheat. They have, say, a sixty-page report to transmit and the way to do it is to break it into forty or so one-time codes, breaking off after so many pages and then inventing the new code. Well, there is a machine that everyone is talking about but no one has yet which is the mother of all code machines. It's a supercomputer that is a perpetual one-time pad. It can change the code every line if need be. Yet the operator can't cheat because the machine does all the work. A machine like that would make cryptography just about foolproof. That's the machine that everyone wants and that Mickey Connors wants. And now I think it's the reason I'm sent in to get on Mickey's team. Because Pendleton wants the machine and he knows the person who's going to get it for him."

"Mickey Connors."

"Eventually. Or possibly. No, it's Denisov."

She knew the name of the man. Denisov had been sent to Florida once to get the secrets of an old priest who had seen too many things in the jungles of Southeast Asia. Rita had met Devereaux then for the first time. Denisov had been sent to kill either Rita or Devereaux or whoever stood in the way of getting the old man's memoirs. Yes. She knew the name.

"Denisov has the machine?"

"Denisov is getting the machine. That's what Mickey Connors says. I don't believe very much of what he says but he has a name and a place and he says that Denisov was making arrangements in Hawaii a few weeks ago—"

"The machine is in Hawaii?"

He looked at her. She was all eagerness now; the face of the reporter being told a story. Why was he telling her? Because, for a very long time in his secret life, he was able to bear the burden of secrecy alone but she had changed all that. She had given him love when it was the last thing he had ever expected to receive from another person. God, he loved her.

"Probably not. He's talked to a fellow in the drug trade, with a fast boat, named Peterson. That's not important. We're not interested in Hawaii, only in the end result. When Denisov gets the machine and when he tries to sell it."

"To whom? The CIA?"

"No. He can't. He's our . . . asset. But R Section doesn't buy stolen goods. Pendleton can't get around that. We can't deal directly with someone like Denisov and Denisov wouldn't deal with us directly because he'd be afraid of us. We couldn't have a defected Russian KGB agent sell us stolen goods and then live to tell the story, could we?"

"God, this is bad, Dev. This is really bad. And you walked into it for Pendleton."

"I have to do it," Devereaux said. "I don't know that Pendleton just wants the machine. Maybe he wants Mickey Connors to work for him. Maybe, maybe."

"Mickey Connors could be trusted but Denisov couldn't trust R Section."

Devereaux spread his hands on the table and looked at the stretched fingers and spoke to his hands. "Section can't be blackmailed." He paused. "Mickey Connors is a crook, essentially. Denisov can deal with a crook and be that much removed by the crook. And Section can deal with a crook but not a defected spy who does illegal things. I mean, this machine does not belong to the United States government."

"But if they get it, they don't have to tell anyone."

"Yes."

"And Denisov wouldn't know who this Mickey Connors would sell it to."

"Yes."

She got up, restless as a runner waiting for a race. She paced to the window and looked at the forest behind the building. She spoke to the glass. "I can go to Hawaii. Interview this Peterson. Learn about him."

"No. You must not," he said.

"Why not?"

"Because. No matter what happens, there'll be bad along the trail."

"Who's making the machine?"

"I don't know," he lied.

"How will Denisov steal it?"

"I don't know. But whoever he steals it from will be after

him. On the trail of it. And no one caught on the trail is going to be alive for very long."

"You're saying that to scare me."

"Be scared, Rita. You can always be scared."

"And what if you get out of this alive, Dev? Do you wait until the next time and the next time? Do we always have to go through this? I can't live apart from you. I thought you knew that. I thought we had worked that out."

They made love. They were so lost and so abandoned that the softness of making love filled in the hollow places in them. They made love in the intense and selfish way of people who have been held apart a long time. When he satisfied her and put his hands under her, pushed up her body to meet him more deeply, he satisfied himself. He wanted to lick her face in the comforting way that some animals lick their beloved. When he was exhausted, they slept a little and there were no dreams in his sleep. When he awoke, it was sudden. It was night. He didn't know where he was. And then he felt her next to him and he felt an indescribable sadness. Because it was time now to leave her again.

FOURTEEN

Mickey Connors picked up the phone in the back room. The telephone had no number on it and was not connected in any way to the telephone at the bar in front. His telephone had not even been installed by the telephone company, though it used company lines. It was untappable because it didn't exist. He dialed a number; he preferred dials on telephones and whiskey drunk straight and boxer shorts and a number of other set and precise things that you might not have expected in a seemingly unfussy man.

"So what'd he do?" he began without greeting.

"He was booked on United and then on Delta. He took Delta to Atlanta and turned around and took Delta to Washington. Our fella saw him get on the D.C. plane and he called the man down there."

"Good fella," Mickey said.

"The fella caught the cab number and we made a cabbie

twenty bucks richer an hour later. He went to the apartment."

"And she was there."

"Well, we figure so. He left an hour ago and the lights were on. And then they went out so she's up there. She was there, ninety percent certain."

"That's love for ya, ain't it?"

"I wouldn't know," the voice said. "After that, he goes to Dulles and catches a red-eye out to San Francisco. So he's not going through LAX at all."

"He's a devious fella, Devereaux. Well, you can't blame him and the girl for missin' each other, I suppose."

"What do you want to do with him?"

"Ah, there's time, there's time, Tommy. Never tap the tree till the sap's ready to burst. Plenty of time to figure out things."

"You wanta watch him at the other end. I can call up to San Fran—"

"Naw, naw. He's not gonna go anywhere but right where I told him to go. The thing is about the girlie, Rita Macklin. What d'ya think he might of told her, her being a newspaperwoman and all."

"You wanna do somethin' there?"

"We don't harm women, Tommy. There's nothin' to do."

"You can make an exception."

"If I was to do that, Tommy, you'd lose respect. For me and yerself. Shut your gob, now, Tommy."

Silence on the line. Mickey was thinking and he didn't realize he was smiling as well.

"Well, the thing about her is we gotta watch her. I want a couple of men, good fellas now and not some boys from the force out to make a little extra money on the side. Good fellas. Just watch her and you call up the bar when you got somethin' to say."

He broke the connection.

FIFTEEN

Devereaux got a room on the fifth floor of the sand-colored hotel on Cabrillo Boulevard. The hotel was across the street from the beach and the grounds were California-immaculate with grass that never seemed to grow or to become brown, spotted with little palm trees and shrubs cut into alarming shapes.

Denisov lived on Alisos up the hill and across Highway 101 from the hotel.

Devereaux knew the building and he knew the habits of the Russian. There would be a morning walk, there was probably a chess club somewhere, and there would be those soulful strolls along the beachfront when Denisov communed with the oil derricks poking up through the waters of the Santa Barbara Channel.

Except that everything was out of the ordinary.

Denisov did not leave the apartment building until ten in

the morning most days and he left with a woman each time. The woman was tan and fit and disturbingly familiar. Her hair was cut short and her eyes were large, with brown pupils that seemed to swim at the edge of tears.

What Rita had said was not true; Devereaux had forgotten.

The first night in California, Devereaux called Dougherty's and tried to leave his telephone number. The barman said, "I'll tell him you was looking for him."

"You take a number?"

"I look like an answering service?" And hung up.

Devereaux had smiled at the rudeness and the aura of secrecy Connors was surrounded with. Some of it seemed absurd caution.

But what had been more absurd than his own devious route back to Rita in Bethesda . . . only to tell her the broad outlines of a secret assignment? Because she had gone to Pendleton and because that put her in danger of becoming part of this. Or of Pendleton telling her the blackmail. That was the thing Devereaux feared most. It would have had an effect, the opposite of what Pendleton intended, and it would have started to ruin their lives, both of their lives, for the rest of their lives.

He thought about the woman with Denisov. It had stirred a memory and yet he could not find the face in the file. He spent the first three days only watching, trying to fill in what person Denisov had become. He had been very set in simple ways before and now he was at the center of a dangerous new game that involved at least two government agencies and a foreign company and two ruthless middleman organizations that made their livings by doing the dirty acts that even government agencies couldn't admit to doing.

What had changed in Denisov.

The woman, the woman. He felt a vague stirring of memory but it was so indistinct. It might have been in Asia, it might have been one of the nurses from the hospital in Saigon. . . .

It might have been anyone in any of a thousand places all crammed into his mind like photographs stashed in a shoebox.

He could not remember.

And then, one afternoon, the woman left the apartment alone. He had been watching from a café on the corner and his small, anonymous Honda was parked outside the window.

The woman got into a red Toyota and started away. He hadn't come to watch the woman but some instinct drove him now to rise and leave a couple of dollars on the table and start for the door.

She took Highway 101 west through the pretty, jeweled city of whitewashed buildings and red tile roofs. The highway curved into the hills and climbed and then fell toward the Santa Barbara airport on the ocean.

She had no bag with her.

She was meeting someone.

She drove to the terminal and parked in a no-parking zone.

He followed her to the baggage claim area beneath the main level. And then he understood.

It was Ruth. The little waif on the train platform in Paris so long ago. The girl who had insisted on making love to him and had left him to die in a brothel in Zurich's old town.

Because now she was holding the man and kissing him and it was Kurt Heinemann. He would never forget the face or the scar or the black, wild eyes. Ruth had changed over the years but Kurt Heinemann was exactly the same as the photograph in Devereaux's memory. He had shot Devereaux in that room and the next thing he had known, he was in a hospital in Zurich and Pendleton was there and . . .

And Pendleton was there. Now Devereaux was in Santa

Barbara working for a crook, trying to steal a secret code machine of some kind from someone.

He stood by a bank of pay telephones and watched their meeting in the middle of the baggage claims area. She handed him an envelope and he handed her a much larger envelope. They talked but Devereaux wasn't close enough to hear them. And then she kissed him again, on the cheek, and he turned and he waved at her and was striding away, probably back to another plane. Or perhaps a private plane.

He followed Ruth back to the apartment building on Alisos but it was done automatically because she had no idea he was following her and because he knew exactly where she would go back.

What more did Pendleton want from him?

Devereaux took a long shower. The water felt good and he could close his eyes and just feel the water and let the thoughts come, jumbled, out of order and rank, thoughts that mixed up the past and present. All his past life in Section tumbled down into this California city, fell in the shower of water in this hotel room.

He turned off the water and stepped out of the tub and stood in the steam of the small bathroom. He stared at the man in the foggy mirror and then wiped a circle of the glass and looked at his face. What was he looking for? But he wasn't sure at all.

He dried himself with the thick, white towels and padded into the bedroom. He dialed the number in New York again and he said Mickey's name.

"Who are you?" the barman said.

He said his name.

"Where you at? You didn't leave a number."

He smiled at that. He gave the number.

"Tell Mickey," he said.

"I look like his answering service?" Hung up. The same old lines, same old tired saloon with the iron resistance to anything and anyone outside that world. Hell's Kitchen, very much that.

The telephone rang an hour later.

Devereaux picked it up and waited.

"See anything interesting?"

"Not yet," Devereaux said.

"You wouldn't hold out on me."

"You can fire me when you want."

"Is that a fact? I wonder what would happen if I did. What about Denisov, what's he doing?"

"He walks a lot, plays chess. He's got a girlfriend who sleeps with him."

"What's her name?"

"I don't know. I haven't been here that long."

"So he's got a girlfriend. Everyone should have a girlfriend. How you holdin' up, you think you might get back with your girl?"

"Things happen sometimes."

"Did she throw out your clothes?"

Devereaux blinked. Mickey didn't care if Devereaux now knew the phone in Rita's apartment was tapped. And that Mickey had heard their conversation that night he called her from the Croydon Hotel. The night Mickey had decided that Devereaux might be bona fide. Mickey was getting careless or Mickey didn't have to care. Something had changed between them and Devereaux felt it over 2,500 miles of telephone line.

"Probably gave them to a charity. She isn't much on wasting things," he said.

"You dress kind of crummy anyway. There probably wasn't much there."

"I'll use your tailor next time I'm in New York," Devereaux said. "I told you this was the wrong way to work it. I'm just standing around looking at a fat Russian go through his daily life without a clue. You should be looking at Consortium in Denver. The spy tell you anything more?"

"Not much," Mickey said, cautious as a cardplayer. "Nothing you can use."

Devereaux was silent. Mickey was edging around again, he could hear it in the voice. Something didn't fit right now and it had all changed since he left New York that morning.

"Maybe the girl is the clue. *La femme.* Lemme know."

"I got any way to reach you at all?"

"As long as I can reach you," Mickey Connors said, and broke the connection.

SIXTEEN

Rita Macklin had spent the morning at Pearl Harbor where the dead ship *Arizona* rested in the shallow water. It was supposed to be one of the reasons for her trip. She had sold Mac on this story and another story and not told him the truth at all. It was not the first time she had lied to her editor at the magazine but it was the first time she had done it for this reason.

He had shared part of a secret.

She had tried to see it in the warm, still water of Pearl Harbor where the ship *Arizona* was in a shallow, wet grave, marked with a memorial to the bones of the sailors entombed inside. She was a reporter and watcher and she tried to see the past in the stillness of the present. It sometimes worked, to stand perfectly still and see the faces and hear the sounds of other times long dead. It is not true that you have to experience a thing to feel it because all the dead of all the battles never leave the battleground. They remain there as ghosts above the graves, waiting to touch the kindred spirits of the living.

In the afternoon, she met the man in the café of the Holiday Inn where she stayed off Waikiki Beach. His name was Ernie Funo, a Japanese-American whose parents had been interred in California in the first years of the war. He was as tall as she and powerfully built with thick, dark hair framing an open face with just the trace of a mocking smile on his lips. He worked as a stringer for the same magazine that employed Rita Macklin and he aspired to more. He knew his way around the islands and he knew some secrets that never show up in print. He knew about a man named Captain Peterson.

She slipped into a chair opposite him and waited for coffee. He had his in front of him, along with a copy of the *New York Times* turned to the crossword puzzle. He gave her a rueful smile because his head hurt. They had seen the nightlife of Honolulu the night before and it was much like the nightlife in other cities, where excess is turned into a cause for celebration.

"You look like a walking hangover," she said. She liked him from the first. He was quick and he knew the things she wanted to know for herself.

"Cheerfulness at the beginning of the day signifies a bad end," he said. The coffee came along with menus.

They ordered food. The waitress walked away and Funo looked at her and the mocking smile was back again, brushing against the hangover in his eyes.

"Peterson went out this morning."

"Is that unusual?"

"He went out alone. His ship, *Pequod*, is a thirty-six-footer and he can handle it, but it's odd. If he's making a big drug pickup, he would take along some of the gang. But he went alone and that's odd and it's odd where he went."

"Where was that?"

"I talked to a fellow named Jimmy Wong. A nice fellow except for his cocaine habit. I spent a hundred dollars to help supply him. From company funds."

"Keep a receipt," she said.

"Yes. But I don't think the IRS will approve. Anyway. Jimmy was out this morning himself, he wouldn't say why but I can guess. He was out ten miles and saw the *Pequod* going flat-out due west. Maybe Peterson is going to Japan."

Japan. She kept the excitement out of her face by staring at the coffee as she carefully stirred it.

"What's this really about, Rita?"

Exactly as Devereaux would say it. She had lied to Funo from the beginning because he wasn't part of this, Mac wasn't part of this, Devereaux would have said she wasn't part of this.

"We're going to do a major on the Asian drug trade. And Hawaii is part of it."

"Peterson is a low-life beginning to a big story."

"Where was he going?"

"I don't know."

She glanced at him. He was waiting for something and so was she.

"You've got some idea."

"Peterson is a smuggler and that means dope because that's what people usually smuggle. But there have been other things smuggled."

"What things?"

"I read five newspapers every day. It's part of my job. At least, the way I see my job. I like the patterns in stories. You can tell things beyond the stories themselves if you read the patterns the right way. Do you know what I mean?"

"Yes. But I don't read five newspapers."

"Perhaps you have a more active life than I do. Look here. There was a story on the inside pages of the *Times* four days ago. A freighter blew up in the Sea of Japan called the *Fujitsu*. I was a little intrigued and I got a copy of the *Asahi Shimbum* for the next day and they made quite a story out of it, bigger than the *Times*'s first story. The ship had twenty in the crew and they recovered thirteen bodies. The ship went down in two hours and it belonged to Masatata Heavy Industries.''

''What's that?''

''The usual conglomerate. They make bicycles and auto parts and everything between. The last five years, they've built an enormous R & D facility in Hokkaido in the north. Very secure. They even use some Tokyo gangsters for security, which shows they're serious. The spokesman for Masatata says the ship contained computers.''

Computers. She held her breath and he noticed it and a small, knowing smile replaced the mocking smile. ''This is about computers, isn't it, Rita? You just didn't want to tell me.''

''What was really on the ship that blew up?''

''Computers.'' Funo shrugged. ''I don't know. I do know that the first ship on the scene arrived less than an hour after she went down. It was a Soviet trawler, the *Novostok*. But everyone was dead. The sea was rough.''

''There's life-saving equipment—''

''Exactly. But there wasn't anything in the water. Not a raft, not a preserver. Everything went down. That makes it a mystery.''

''What's the connection to *Pequod* and Peterson?''

Funo smiled then. ''I have a friend named Toshibata at *Shimbum* in Tokyo and I called him. Very expensive call, I kept a receipt. I asked him some more because I like to watch things and anything about Japanese business makes news in America. He told me a second ship could have reached the *Fujitsu* before it went down. It was a freighter called the *Northern Lights*, it's an American ship registered in the Bahamas but it works down the Aleutians this time of year to warm water. Does coasting and some transshipping to the warm-water Alaskan ports in winter like Haines. But I checked with the shipping desk at the *Advertiser* and they said the *Northern Lights* is headed due east for Hawaii. And the *Lights* has never put in at Hawaii. Do you see the connection?"

She shook her head. "Too many connections, Ernie. You're dreaming up a story—"

He flushed then. "Not really. The *Northern Lights* has been involved in smuggling too, in Alaskan waters. Boom, there's an accident and boom, there's a ship on the scene that heads for Hawaii and then, boom boom, a known local smuggler called Peterson goes out to meet it. What do you think?"

"None of this is in the newspapers."

"What we know and what we print are different things sometimes, Rita." He was smiling again. "I called Mifuno again just a little while ago and he said the word among the gangsters in Tokyo is that they're going after the *Northern Lights*. Why? Did the *Northern Lights* pick up a waterlogged computer? Or is it something else?" He paused. "Tell what else it is, Rita."

But she was thinking out loud. "Peterson will come back into Honolulu."

"Yes."

"And the shipping authorities—"

"The port police and DEA will take him apart. They'll look for cocaine or even marijuana. Something that Peterson deals in. The port is very strung-out today, the dopies think Peterson was out getting medicine to make them feel better."

"But they won't find what they're looking for," Rita Macklin said.

"That's what I think. And I'll bet the *Northern Lights* turns north tomorrow after dropping off a package to a certain party in midocean."

"Back to Alaska."

"Rita, we can meet Peterson when he comes in. Interview him and look around if you want. But you've got to tell me more than you told me because you're not looking at Peterson for a drug-smuggling story."

She bit her lip. It was a pretty gesture because she had a slight overbite and because she did this in the way of a woman who is thinking furiously beyond the present conversation.

"I can't tell you anything, Ernie. If you have to back out, you have to back out, but this is about something else, something you don't want to know anything about."

It was something that Devereaux might have said.

SEVENTEEN

1 Oct 90—DENVER

Pendleton met him in room 569 at precisely four in the afternoon. It was that important to both of them, to make sure there was no misunderstanding and no telephone contact. Pendleton came alone into Stapleton on a regular commercial flight and he took a cab to two other hotels before transferring to a third cab and ending up at the airport Hilton. Heinemann had been just as circumspect.

Pendleton grinned at Heinemann when he entered the room. The German agent was as pale as ever, his white scar etched in an unnatural shade of white against his skin, a speck of paint on the skin.

Pendleton's shirt was soaked with sweat. He always sweated on airplanes, always adjusted the overhead fan, always felt used up by a trip at thirty thousand feet. He was the born man in control and it unnerved him to think that someone else might have control over his safety and destiny, even for three hours of his life.

"Did you have a good flight?" The question was asked with irony.

"They're all good," Pendleton said, annoyed. He carried a single case and flopped it on the bed and began to take off his jacket. And then stopped. He looked at Heinemann. "Hungry." He walked to the phone. "Never eat airplane food and you live to be a hundred."

Heinemann stared at him and Pendleton smiled. He was the center of attention again.

"Yeah," he said into the phone. "Room 569. Want something to eat. Lemme see. A cheeseburger medium. Fries. Some beer. You got some Heineken?" Covered the phone. "You want a beer?"

Heinemann shook his head.

"Four Heineken and I want them in an ice bucket, I don't want beer just sitting there on a tray. Cold Heineken. That's right." He was enjoying himself because Kurt Heinemann was standing there, waiting for a man in shirtsleeves to order lunch. Pendleton wanted to make the other man wait and it was one of the small, annoying tricks of his trade. He annoyed people over trivialities and this allowed him to take advantage of them. At least, Pendleton believed this about himself.

It was only their third meeting in less than a year, from the moment when Kurt Heinemann had become the agent—the personal agent—of the director of operations for R Section.

When Kurt began his fill-in, Pendleton held up his hand. "I want to wash up and change my shirt. I hate to wear a shirt that's been on an airplane for three hours."

Another petty thing and Kurt understood this about Pendleton and had observed it first fifteen years before when he had sold out a Soviet spy network to Pendleton. When it came down to it, Pendleton held up his end of the bargain but that wouldn't be the case here. No, Pendleton was going to have this blow up in his face and he would know it, even if he never had to tell a soul about it.

Pendleton came out of the washroom and was buttoning his clean shirt. He dumped the other shirt in the wastebasket under the desk. He was smiling at the German.

"How's it going in Denver? Dull town. Pretty but dull. You like it okay?"

"Maybe I like dull," Heinemann said. "There's enough excitement in the world."

"Is there enough excitement?"

They stared at each other.

"The business comes down in two days. I will buy the code machine from Denisov."

"Two days."

"*Ja.*"

Pendleton shook his head and smiled. "Two days. Can't believe it, coming down to the end, all these months. Tell you the truth, when you first came to me with this shit about Denisov, I couldn't believe it."

Heinemann stared at the large man. His eyes were cold, reflecting no curiosity, only a dull patience.

"You wanted out of East Germany so bad, I thought maybe you made it up. Then I did my own snooping. There were rumors about a machine, even back last year. We deal in rumors, don't we? I mean, you shopped me some tidbit and I bit on it. I thought you just wanted out."

"I wanted a safe haven. And we did business, *Herr Direktor*. In Zurich a long time ago. We kept the . . . bargain."

"That's what I thought, took a chance on. Took a chance on you, Kurt."

Kurt made a sallow smile. He nodded. "*Danke, Herr Direktor.*"

"You better *danke*," Pendleton said. Stopped. The cold thing came over his blue eyes. He was a bastard all right, Heinemann thought. He enjoyed the role.

The food came. Cheeseburgers dripping with grease and French fries that were soggy and cold. And bottles of Heineken in an ice bucket.

"You want a beer first, Kurt?"

"I don't drink beer."

"Must be some strange kraut not to drink beer. Cheers." Pendleton was in a good mood.

"You want the fill now, *Herr Direktor*?" he said with sarcasm and Pendleton caught it but the little smile on his lips made it all right. He liked to annoy Kurt Heinemann because it meant Kurt Heinemann was in his power. They all were, even the difficult ones like Devereaux who thought they had their own law inside Section. Pendleton was changing all that, changing the way things were done and the way thinking was done inside R Section.

Pendleton nodded.

The fill was nearly all true. There was the matter of Miss Browning first.

Kurt Heinemann stated it cleanly: "I determined how much she knew and who she gave this to. Then I eliminated her."

"How'd you do that?"

"It was done."

"I like the gory details."

Kurt stared at the hamburger, at the soggy French fries. Yes. The gory details.

"She was frightened, not much more than an amateur. She worked for Mickey Connors in New York. She didn't get to pass along much, just the rumors about a machine, a code machine that Consortium wanted. She kept calling me

Mr. Dodge, even when I hurt her. She had no idea of what I was."

"How'd you hurt her?"

"The most efficient way."

"How's that?"

He took no pleasure in this but he saw that Pendleton did. Another matter of control. He made a face and walked to the window. He looked down at the sun-bathed streets clogged with traffic. Interstate 70 was backed up for at least a mile, every car containing some frustrated driver who was eating up the minutes of his life trapped in metal and the vagaries of the afternoon rush hour.

"I cut her wrist. It doesn't hurt very much but there is a lot of blood and it frightens them. They realize it is their blood. They tell you everything very quickly or they'll never tell you anything. She wanted to save her life."

"But she didn't."

"I shot her, very close, there was no pain."

"That's too bad," Pendleton said. He was smiling at Kurt. "And what about the toy, this machine?"

"Denisov. He wants to see me in two days, it is that close."

"Two days. The third."

"At three. We make the transfer. Gandolph is collecting the money."

"Gandolph is gonna be a good man for Section."

"What do I do?"

"Friday. Then what?"

"*Ja*, then what, *Herr Direktor*? What do I do?"

"You bury the code machine when you get it from Denisov and you go to Mr. Gandolph and you tell him that he is now going to sell it to R Section for exactly fifteen million dollars and if he thinks he can double-cross you, you tell him that you're my agent and we can blow Consortium International to kingdom come, is what you tell him. You got that Kurt?"

"*Ja.*" It was along the lines of what he thought.

"Gandolph is not a dumb man," Pendleton said, chewing loudly. "I set you up with him in the first place. He was willing to take a flyer on you and he thinks he might be able to have it both ways, deal with R Section, keep his hand in dealing with Langley. All he could see was that code machine, he really wants it. The brilliant thing you brought to this was knowing how to find the man who was going to steal. Finding Denisov. When you told me it was Denisov last summer, I about shit. Denisov was a name out of the past. Gandolph may think he can string me along until you get the machine from Denisov. Then maybe he'll revert to type and sell it to Langley. He isn't going to do that, is he, Kurt?"

Kurt shook his head. It was what Pendleton wanted, physical punctuation marks for his pronouncements.

"No sir, Kurt. Langley's got no piece of this. They buzz around and they can smell the horseshit but they can't get near it. Denisov was defected by us, he's our asset, and they can't touch him. Even if Langley thinks Denisov is going to deal in something. You got to convince Gandolph that he only deals with us or I'll go after Consortium International with a pitchfork. Make a lot of holes."

"Gandolph will be handled," Kurt said, thinking of something else.

"I want Consortium in my camp. Working for me, same as you. Give him the code machine when you get it from Denisov and then make him give it to me."

It was boring, Kurt thought. The same message said in different ways. He went to the window and looked out so that he would not have to look at the man eating his cheeseburger.

"Another thing now. Just so you don't think you're out there alone, Kurt."

Waited, his back turned to Pendleton.

"Gandolph has a rival he knows about. An Irish fellow, a crook out of New York. A bastard named Mickey Connors. I been setting him up since you told me it was Denisov. Our defected Russian agent living a life of retirement in sunny Santa Barbara."

He had not heard of this.

"Mickey Connors got himself another one of my special . . . employees. You know him."

Kurt had to turn. Pendleton was grinning at him with a mouthful of food. He chewed it down and the grin never varied.

"Devereaux."

Kurt shook his head.

"Yeah. You know him. The man you shot in Zurich that one time. I bet he hasn't forgot you, Kurt. He's working for Mickey Connors and they're working on the same thing. Mickey Connors is another middleman. Does jobs for CIA all over. Sells arms. Probably runs guns to the rebels in Ireland. Devereaux came along at the right time for Mickey Connors because Mickey heard about Denisov making a purchase. I don't know if they know all about a code machine but they know it's something."

"Where is Devereaux?" Kurt Heinemann said.

"In Santa Barbara. He's watching Denisov. That gives you a problem."

Kurt stared at the large man as Pendleton opened another green bottle of beer. He watched the beer fill a glass.

"It gives me a problem," Kurt said.

"He could complicate things, couldn't he?"

"You know this? Why didn't you tell me before?"

"Because Devereaux is no problem. He's right where I want him."

"He can interfere—"

"He will be left holding the bag, Kurt. Our man in California, working for an arms trader, making a deal with the agent he defected for us ten years ago. Devereaux and Denisov are two peas and I got them right in the pod. Denisov was Devereaux's property, his big catch in all his years as an agent. Natural that Devereaux is working now for Mickey Connors's gang and since they're business rivals of Consortium, Mickey is using Devereaux." Tasted the beer. "We're going to use him too."

"How?"

"Kill him. When the deal is ready to go down in two days, you kill him. I'll put the fear on Gandolph with him. Give you a club to use. You kill Devereaux and you show Gandolph how close it was, how a renegade agent from Section was working for Mickey Connors against you. It'll be enough to tip him if you need it. Mickey Connors works for Langley too and Gandolph is going to figure that Langley bypassed its usual channels with CI to get the code machine that Denisov is selling. That Langley put Mickey Connors on the trail to outfox you."

"But did they?"

"In a funny way. Mickey Connors knows some things and Langley knows other things. They keep a casual eye from time to time on all our . . . assets. They want to know what we're doing as much as we want to know what they're doing. Denisov is no secret to Langley but they won't go near him. That's the rules. We don't poach on each other's territory. Denisov belongs to us. That's why you're a wild card. No one except Gandolph knows you have connections to me and Gandolph isn't advertising it. You're just a German ex-agent and the last person in the world that Langley would expect to be making the deal with Denisov. See how neat it is?"

"Devereaux knows me." And didn't say that Devereaux knew Ruth as well.

"Devereaux is tied up in knots. I put him in deep cover to infiltrate the Connors gang. He doesn't know what he's doing but he keeps doing it because he has to. He called me. I got his location. I'm going to give it to you, Kurt, right down to his room number in Santa Barbara. You can fix him when you make your deal with Denisov."

"Why do this thing? This complicates everything."

"It gets me two birds with one stone. Maybe four. One, I get rid of a pain in the ass named Devereaux. He doesn't trust me, never has since Zurich, and I don't like to look over my shoulder and see him. Second, I cripple up Mickey Connors because when Langley finds out—and they'll find out—that Connors was using a Section agent and got nothing to show for it, they'll start wondering how far to trust him. I got no use for Connors. Irish crooks, renegades."

"You said four things," Kurt said.

"Third: Consortium. I build a new relationship with a useful organization. And last, I get the code machine. I want the code machine."

"You said it wasn't that important."

"When I picked you up at the airport last Christmas. Sure it's important. Just like you're important to me, Kurt."

"You're too devious, there are too many things that can go wrong. You complicate too much."

"Don't tell me my job. Don't ever do that—"

"And me, boss. What about me?"

"You stay as you are. A guest of the nation. Work for Consortium. Work with Gandolph. Make money and have a good life. Do your dirty tricks for profit and for me. I need someone who needs me." Smiled. "You need me in the worst way, Kurt, that's why I can trust you. You need every protection I can give you. The world thinks Kurt Heinemann went to Moscow when East Germany collapsed but we know different."

There it was. His future. Pendleton's puppet.

He wanted to kill him in that moment.

The anger passed. There was no time for anger. He would

not be a puppet too much longer. He would kill Denisov and now he would kill Devereaux as well. And Gandolph, that was important. And then he would be gone with fifteen million dollars to set up a new network in Germany and a code machine that would fetch at least that much more. Not for himself, not for riches, but for a new order of things that would not depend on the stupidity of the Russians. Made in Germany with German hands.

"Why are you smiling, Kurt?"

Soft question.

Kurt didn't realize he was smiling. He looked at the director of Operations of R Section, the man who had brought him in from the cold.

And left him in a different kind of cold.

"I was thinking of Devereaux," Kurt lied.

"You like the idea of taking him out."

"*Ja, ja,*" Kurt said. "I like that you had to save him once in Zurich to take the blame of that . . . trade we made. And the dead Mossad agents. I liked that then and now you are doing the same thing, letting him mislead Langley this time into a setup against this Connors man."

"Only now we kill him," Pendleton said.

"*Ja.* The only difference is that now he dies."

EIGHTEEN

It followed a familiar script. Two policemen and an agent from the Drug Enforcement Administration were waiting at the dock as the *Pequod* rumbled slowly through the oily waters to harbor.

The white yacht had rust patches here and there. It was wide and high with a deep draft for ocean use. Peterson was alone, his face calm and eyes shining with liquor, as he stood on the pilot deck and nudged the boat cleanly to its place on the dock. He threw out lines to a couple of idlers on the dock and climbed down. He crossed to the rail. He threw the sailors two rolls of quarters that bounced on the deck.

The policeman asked to look at the rolls.

"Make sure they don't steal from you lads. Count your quarters." Peterson grinned. The smile was as crooked as everything else about him.

"We're coming aboard," the DEA man said. He held a piece of paper in his hand.

Peterson grinned. "Is that you, Keller? I'm sorry to keep you up so late, I know you like to be home in bed by ten o'clock. That's G-man hours."

Keller shoved a gangplank to the opening in the bow and walked across. His eyes were dead with vacant contempt. Peterson looked over the rail at the two policemen still on the dock. And then he saw the red-haired woman and the Oriental man, standing in the glare of a lamppost.

"Hey, honey, you. What are you?"

"I'm a reporter, I want—"

"Can it, Peterson, lead the way," Keller said. One of the policemen followed the DEA man onto the boat and the second stood at the gangplank and glared at Rita Macklin and Ernie Funo.

Peterson smiled at the woman and then let the smile fade when he turned to Keller. They started below, the smuggler leading the way.

It took a half hour. They went through the decks and tore up sheets and the beds and pulled out all the drawers. And then they were back on deck again, Peterson glaring now because the boat was a mess.

"This is fucking harassment," he was saying, "Every time I come in, you got a hard-on for me—"

"I got a hard-on for you," Keller said. "And someday it's gonna stick you."

"I'll get a court order."

"Sure," the federal man said. "You show me the order sometime because I'll be back, Peterson."

The cops climbed back into their cars and crept off the dock and the reporters moved forward to the gangplank still in place.

"Well, pretty lady, what can I do for you?"

Rita walked up the gangplank to the edge of the deck

and stopped. She had pressed the button on her tape recorder.

"You could tell me what you're smuggling. I don't suppose you would."

He grinned at her. Funo stood at the base of the plank.

"I know you, don't I? You're Ernie Funo. You're another fucking reporter, aren't you? You sic the cops on me this time, Ernie?"

"You sic them on yourself when you disappear at dawn all alone in your boat," Funo said.

"Nobody's got a right to interfere with nobody. Including journalists."

"My name is Rita Macklin. I'm doing a story on smuggling in the islands."

"Really? What would you want with me? You've probably been listening to Funo, he's full of shit. He thinks he knows what's going on but he don't. Not any more than those clowns in uniform."

"Tell me about smuggling," she said.

"Who you work for?"

She told him.

"I canceled my subscription, but if you promise to spell my name right, I wouldn't mind getting in your story. That kind of attention draws people. Fishermen with big wallets who like to go out with a real smuggler. The way you'll make me out in your story."

"You are a smuggler, aren't you?" Rita smiled at him.

"Smuggling is an honorable trade but I don't say I'm a smuggler, just that's what you'll say I am. You want to step aboard, lady, take a cup of sunshine with just a poor old broken-down sailor?"

Funo took a step on the gangplank and Peterson held up his hand.

"Invitation for one. For the pretty lady, Ernie Funo, not you."

"Don't go, Rita," Funo said, and took another step. But Rita had already stepped on deck. "It's all right, Ernie. Wait for me."

The cabin was large. It had been neat until all the drawers were pulled out. Peterson swept a clear space on the table with the side of his arm. Rita took out her camera and snapped a picture while he pulled down a bottle of Early Times. He opened the bottle and poured some into two glasses. He looked around. "Look at this. They do it all the time, they do it on purpose. Keller likes to rummage the drawers and turn them upside down. That asshole wouldn't be able to find a load of coke if you shoved it up his nose."

"Is that what you smuggle, Mr. Peterson? Cocaine?"

"I was never convicted of anything except that one time. A long time ago and it was nothing."

"What was nothing?"

"I don't deal in cocaine, none of the white trade, honey." He leered at her over the table and then bent and kissed her full on the lips. She shoved him hard and he stumbled back and was still smiling. "I bet you're hot, I bet you can turn it on."

"I want to know about smuggling," she said. Hard.

He was still grinning but now he shrugged at her and took his glass. He tasted the whiskey and made a face and took another swallow.

"I know my way around, that's true." His face was raw with wind and sun. "Everyone knows their way around if they survive at all. The coke trade don't need a ship. Coke is small and easy, you can fly it in easier than you can ship it in. It's all just waterfront talk, every time a ship goes out, they gossip about her. Now take cannabis. There was money in that once for sailors because the stuff was so damned bulky but now it's more work than it's worth. They grow the stuff here, right on the islands, and you'd think Keller could find it. Shit. He probably smokes it himself."

"You used to smuggle marijuana?"

"Did I say that? Did your tape recorder get me to say that? I don't think so, pretty lady. I said I know the waterfront."

"What did you get from the *Northern Lights* today?" she said.

Silence, sudden and dark. He stared at her green eyes and saw they were cold and knowing. He finished his glass of whiskey and poured another.

His hand was not as steady now.

"Turn off that fucking tape recorder," he said.

She clicked it off.

"What kind of a story are you writing?"

"About the thing you smuggled from the *Northern Lights*. And from the *Fujitsu*. That was murder, not smuggling cocaine, Mr. Peterson. Men died on the *Fujitsu*."

"What *Fujitsu* are you talking about?"

"The ship that went down in the Sea of Japan. The *Northern Lights* picked up something—"

"Who the hell are you?"

"I told you."

"You don't work for no fucking magazine—"

"You took stolen goods and that makes you part of the murder. All those men killed on the *Fujitsu*," she said. Her voice was so cold that he could feel it like an icy hand on his chest.

"I didn't kill anyone. You get off my boat."

"I want to know about the computer," she said. She watched him and he couldn't look at her for a moment. Then he turned to her and his eyes were full of rage. "I could slice your liver, girlie, and feed it to the fish."

"Funo. He's right on deck."

"And that slant as well, both of you."

She stood up and stared at him.

"Get off my boat," he said.

"You're going to be in bad trouble before very long," she said.

"What are you, the G? You working with Keller? What the hell is this about?"

"Keller was looking for one thing. I'm looking for something else. You want to talk to me, Peterson, you really do. I'm at the Holiday Inn and you can call me. Talk to me. You really want to talk to me."

"I got nothing to talk to you about."

"All those men drowned. And they're looking for it already and when they find out you've got it, they'll come after you and nobody is going to help you then. But you might have some time if you talk to me." Very cold still, her green eyes like a sea waiting for the storm.

"Get out, get out."

"Remember to call me. Room two-ninety. Rita Macklin."

He heard himself screaming at her but she was already up the ladder to the deck and Funo was suddenly on deck and he helped her down the gangplank. But Peterson would not come up. He was shouting curses at her and her face was white.

"What happened?" Funo said.

She shivered then at the touch of his hand on her sleeve and looked into his eyes. "It's true, Ernie. The damned thing is true and I don't know what to do with it now."

NINETEEN

The telephone call came at midnight. Denisov listened and said nothing and waited for the code word. But the distraught voice on the other end repeated a name over and over. He was drunk. This wasn't any good at all.

"Shut up, Peterson. You have the package. Now get it to me."

"But she knew. The goddamned reporter knew," the voice said. "There's a double-cross going on and you've got me in the middle."

"Get me the package. I have the rest of the money—"

"Money doesn't do me any good if I get sent up for murder."

"There was no murder."

"She said—"

Denisov looked at Ruth across the living room. Midnight and Ruth was a little drunk and very naked. She was sitting

131

with her legs apart on the couch and she was making a lewd gesture with her mouth and tongue. A line of sweat stood out on Denisov's broad forehead but the eyes were clear and calm. As calm as his voice. "It doesn't matter about her." Cold and calm, soothing as ice on a flaming hurt.

Peterson broke the connection.

"Was that the package?" Ruth said.

"The package."

"There's a problem."

"There's no problem."

"Then come here and make love to me," Ruth said. He stared at her. The moment had drained him. Something was wrong but this was such a simple matter; he had spent a year crafting all the corners of the plan, stripping it down to the essentials of the operation and then the final deal. And now a name: Rita Macklin. He thought of Devereaux behind that name. He shivered and went to the couch and began to make love to Ruth Sauer.

Ruth awoke him in the middle of the night with kisses on his belly. Denisov opened his eyes but he did not move. She was kissing him lower and lower and he was stirred by it but he did not believe it was possible. They had made love and then fallen asleep in the bedroom of the small, spare apartment on Alisos. She was her brother's spy and she was a strange lover; she was using him and he was using her and it would end, one way or another, by the end of the week. He didn't trust her at all.

She was licking his skin.

The money had paid for the *Fujitsu* and for the *Northern Lights* and for the *Pequod*. The money had found its way into a Vietnamese network to do the first part of the work and then more of it had found its way into the hands of a ship captain who normally smuggled cocaine into Alaska and then another part into the hands of a petty smuggler in Hawaii.

The Japanese gangsters who protected the secrecy of Masatata H.I. were already following the trail but when they came to the end of it, they would find only a dead German spy and his dead sister. Denisov was quite certain of that. He had always been a careful agent in every secret matter and it was simply a matter of planning. Fifteen million dollars more would buy him a new life as a good burgher in Switzerland. It would buy him his freedom after ten years as a reluctant defector in America. Rita Macklin and the shadow of Devereaux behind her. Why was she in Hawaii at this time and place and why did she know enough to frighten Peterson?

She made him moan. He stirred in bed and she said, "I want you to be inside me."

"Ruth."

It was strange, all of it. To make love to a woman he would have to kill in a little while. He pushed her down on the mattress roughly and put himself over her and they made many sounds that were not words.

Denisov looked at the clock. Three A.M. She was sleeping naked next to him again. He sat up in bed and looked at her. Perhaps she really did love him. Perhaps she was only lonely. She was an exile, the same as he. It was too bad. He touched her brown hair tenderly. He might only kill her brother but that wouldn't be any good. He could never trust her. If he killed Kurt and she stayed alive, there would always be a bond of doubt between them. She was a spy and when her useful time was over, she would have to accept a spy's fate.

He thought of her lovemaking. There was something in it that was more hunger than anything he had ever experienced before.

"Dear little one," he said to her but she was asleep.

He could not sleep anymore. The thought of a woman named Rita Macklin intruded again. He was sweating again. He wiped his forehead.

He threw his legs over the side of the bed and got up. He went to the window and looked down on the empty street, at the sleeping houses of the city.

He would not be sorry to leave. He would have a place in Vevey, in the hills above the city, where he could look at the lake every day.

He pulled on his robe and went into the kitchen. He opened the refrigerator and took out a can of Budweiser. He took the can of beer to the kitchen table and sat down and looked at it for a long time. He was very calm when an operation had begun. He had no doubts about it or himself. There was Kurt; there was Ruth; he could see them in his mind. There was the money; and now, there was the machine. There was no other complication, save that the Japanese company would be sending tracers on the trail that started with the sunken ship in the Sea of Japan, but that was a matter of time. No complication until a midnight call from a drunken man who had the machine and said a name from his past. The woman in California he had once tried to kill. The woman who lived with the agent named Devereaux. He must be right behind her and that meant he must be running toward Denisov.

The kitchen light was fluorescent and the can of beer, still unopened, was sweating.

The apartment was dark. In the darkness beyond the open kitchen, he saw the movement.

That stuck in his throat for a moment, just a moment.

Then he got up and went to the kitchen drawer where he kept the pistol. He opened the drawer.

"Sit down, Russian."

It was really like a dream. He turned and saw the form in the darkness but he could not see the man.

134

And then again: "Sit down."

He went to the table. "Who is there?" But he knew that voice; it had haunted him enough over the past ten years.

"I did never expect to see you again."

"No." Devereaux stepped into the light. He held a pistol in his hand. Denisov looked at the can of beer on the table and at the gun and he was really thinking about the new element, one that did not fit at all.

"Why are you here?" A mild question in a mild voice, as though the intrusion at three in the morning into a locked apartment might not be so unusual.

"It's a good time," Devereaux said. "Call the woman."

"There's no woman here."

"Call her."

He called her name. They waited, staring at each other. Denisov glanced once at the open drawer. Devereaux saw it and slowly shook his head. Denisov sighed and sat down.

Ruth stumbled naked into the kitchen. Her hair was disheveled, her eyes blinking away sleep. When she saw Devereaux, she turned and covered her breasts.

"Hello, Ruth Sauer," Devereaux said. "You're still your brother's whore after all these years."

Then she turned back toward him and dropped her hand and stared at him. "You were the conductor," she said. The voices were all soft, muted by the night, civilized by the barbarity of the hour and occasion.

"He's an American agent," she said to Denisov.

"An American agent," he repeated. Three of them in a still, small room.

"Sit down, Ruth," Devereaux said, and he pointed the pistol at her.

She sat at the table with exaggerated calm, like a drunk pretending to be sober. She stared at the pistol and smiled in a peculiar way.

They both stared at her smile.

She nodded once, to herself, and locked her hands together at the table and gave a small, sharp laugh. "My brother had to kill you to save himself, you know that. I knew that even if he never said it to me. But he didn't kill you. That must be funny."

"You sleep with Denisov for whatever he can give you for your brother," Devereaux said. He was staring at Denisov. "She's the sister of a Stasi agent, Denisov. He wants what you can give him."

"Is that true?" Denisov said. No inflection colored the words of the question.

"It's true," Devereaux said. "You've stolen something and I want it from you."

"I don't have anything. I don't know what you're talking about."

"What about it, Ruth? Where is it?"

"It's not here," Ruth said, still smiling as though listening to another conversation that the two men could not hear. Denisov had never seen her act so strangely. She was staring at Devereaux.

Denisov stared at her. "She doesn't know what she's talking about."

"The package, he wants the package," Ruth said.

"And I want your brother. Where is he now, Ruth?"

The smile finished. Ruth said, "You want to kill him."

"I won't hurt him."

"Yes. Ivan, he was the conductor and he used me, I was just a girl then. Do you know what he made me do for him? And then he wanted to kill my brother. Then. And he wants to kill him now after all these years. He's come all the way from Zurich to kill him."

Silence. They both were staring at the naked woman whose hands were locked on the table and who was now nodding to herself, answering unspoken questions.

"You can't trust him, Ivan," Devereaux said. "Kurt Heinemann is her brother and you think you can sell the code machine to him but he'll kill you. He has to kill you. And take his sister away."

"He can take his sister away at any time," Denisov said in a very calm voice.

Ruth started, looked at him.

"You love me. You said you love me," she said.

"It's not important," Denisov said. He was looking at Devereaux. "What do you propose to me, Devereaux?"

"You give me the code machine," Devereaux said.

"If the machine exists at all."

"You know and I know that it's a matter of time and place now," Devereaux said.

"And if I give you this machine, what will you give me?"

"Your life."

"You've given me my life before. When you defected me," Denisov said. "I should be so grateful to you for another gift that was the same thing."

"Be grateful. Life is a fine gift," Devereaux said.

"Who do you work for now?" Denisov said.

"Section. The same as always."

"No. Not the same. We both know that."

"We both know what?"

"Why are you using Rita Macklin?"

Devereaux said nothing.

"All right. This is no coincidence. What are you willing to pay? And what could be done about Kurt Heinemann?"

The question caused the naked woman to suddenly cry out.

"You bastard, you want to kill Kurt, the same as this . . . this November. That was his name. His name was November and he made me sleep with him on the train, he made me do—"

"Be quiet, Ruth," Devereaux said.

"I'll scream and—"

"And then I'll have to make you quiet," Devereaux said. "Both of you are murderers."

Devereaux said, "Be quiet, Ruth. You did what you could. You whored for your brother again and the customer knew he was getting a whore, nothing more."

Her head shook violently. Again, an arm covered her breasts. "Look at me, you've made me naked."

"Get some clothes," Devereaux said.

She bolted from the table, knocking over her chair, and shut the bedroom door. The two men stared at each other again.

Denisov spoke. "I don't understand your business in this."

"I want what you've got."

"I don't have anything yet. You must know that by now. I'm waiting, the same as you are waiting."

"Where does it come from?"

Denisov almost smiled. "Why play this game with me now? You know everything. You must know there's a price for this code machine. And you must know that Kurt Heinemann is part of the price. But you're not working for Section, are you? You would not show yourself so easy. And the girl, Rita."

"I don't understand," Devereaux said.

"Who do you work for, November? In Section, the method is different. Direct. If you wanted a thing, you would wait for it. But you cannot wait."

"I won't pay your price."

"And what is your price?"

"Why don't you set it."

Denisov stared with mild eyes at the gunman and thought about it. Then he said, "Fifteen million. And Kurt Heinemann."

"Where is she?" Devereaux said, staring at the closed bedroom door. "Ruth."

The door opened.

She was dressed but barely. Her dress was tight and she was obviously naked beneath it. She had her hands behind her, looking like the parody of the frail schoolgirl she had been fifteen years ago on a platform in Paris. She came to the kitchen and stood in front of the man with the pistol. She stood very close to him.

"Do I look as I did?"

Devereaux stared at her and then at Denisov. The atmosphere of the room was charged now with sex and the tension associated with fear.

"Sit down, Ruth."

"I took my dress off in the train and I waited for you to come back. I climbed down the ladder in the compartment and I stood there and you felt me, between my legs. You must remember that."

"I remember your brother shot me."

"He had to shoot you."

"And the two Mossad agents. I killed them for the sake of your terrorist brother."

Very close to him. Her lips were wet and parted. "I loved you," she said.

"You loved me as much as you love Denisov." Silence. "Who do you really love? Kurt? You love the one man who won't sleep with you?"

And then she snarled and her hand swept out suddenly. The knife gleamed in the bright light and slashed up and struck Devereaux's forearm.

He pushed her away with the gun. A spot of blood blossomed on his shirt and it grew but he could scarcely feel the flesh wound.

She screamed at him again and came back with the knife and Denisov reached for the open drawer.

Devereaux shoved, grabbed her wrist and twisted the knife hand and she screamed again, not in rage but pain.

Denisov grasped the pistol in the drawer.

Devereaux twisted the hand and the knife clattered to the floor and then he slammed her shoulder brutally and she fell against the counter. She was breathing hard and so was Devereaux.

Denisov held the pistol very straight, aimed right at Devereaux.

She saw it.

"Kill him," she whispered. "Kill him, Ivan."

Denisov waited. The two men with two guns were facing each other over a four-foot expanse of table.

"Put down the gun," Denisov said.

"I couldn't do that."

"What do we do?"

"Kill him," she snarled again.

Denisov said, "One of us must decide this. If you work for Section, it isn't any good at all."

"We must decide this," Devereaux agreed.

And then Denisov looked at Ruth cringing at the counter. "She can't be trusted at all. It really is too bad. And an irony. Did you sleep with her as well? After fifteen years, we are met and we have both slept with her, the German girl. And she doesn't know who she wants me to kill or even who she is sleeping with, eh?"

Denisov smiled in the middle of his monologue and then turned the pistol slightly and aimed it at Ruth's chest. "She tried to kill you with a little knife."

Devereaux understood but he could not speak.

And Ruth understood in the last moment.

"If you harm me, Kurt will kill you," she said.

"Kurt will try to kill me in any case," Denisov said.

"But you need me, you cannot contact him but through me, you know that."

"But I can't trust you anymore, Ruth," Denisov said.

"You can trust me. I love you, dear one," Ruth said. "Haven't I shown you I love you?"

"Show me now."

And slowly, she came around the table to him, and stood next to him and he took her waist and pulled her close to him. He turned the pistol toward Devereaux again. She made herself small against him.

"You see, it is true. She loves me."

Said without irony.

"And she does not love you."

Devereaux said, "You play your game and I'll play mine."

"But who is it that you work for?"

"I told you."

"I don't believe that. Section does not want toys. Section does not use people like her."

"Like who?"

"Ah, this goes to no place," Denisov said. "If you won't shoot me now, I won't shoot you. Stay away from me unless you can tell me the truth."

"Why won't you shoot me?"

"Tell them the price and see what they will do, but they must do it in a very quick time. Do you understand?"

Devereaux nodded then. He took a step back and then another. They were watching each other. Ruth struggled but Denisov's grip was tight and strong. Devereaux saw the way it was. Denisov wanted another player in the game in case he needed to make a different deal. Ruth had some hold on him, maybe as the contact between Denisov and her brother. But he was frightened, Devereaux thought. He was now very afraid of both Germans.

And so was Devereaux.

TWENTY

Ernie Funo heard the glass break and opened his eyes just as the men entered his bedroom. They wore black suits, white shirts, dark ties and hats. The hats seemed odd and old-fashioned.

The tall one spoke very quickly and harshly in Japanese and the other pulled Funo out of the bed. The clock read 3:01 in the morning.

"I can't speak Japanese that quickly," Funo said.

"My name is Ito," said the shorter one. "You and a white woman went to a ship this night. Where is the master of the ship and where is the white woman?"

"I don't know what you mean, I'm a journalist—"

Ito slashed him then across the belly. The knife was so sharp that there was no pain at first, none at all. And then the pain came in a sickening wave. Funo instinctively grasped his belly and felt blood on his hands.

His eyes were filled with terror.

Ito said, "We don't have time for this. You were part of the theft of the machine. This was very dishonorable."

"I didn't steal anything—" Funo said.

"You and a white woman. And this captain. You paid money to a drug addict to ask about the captain so you know the sea captain was gone to accept a shipment."

"I don't know anything, I just made a guess, I—"

"You talked to two men in Tokyo, on newspapers about our organization and about the shipment of machines by Masatata. We have no more time to waste with you. Where is the white woman and the sea captain?"

Harsh silence. Funo moaned. His hands could not hold in the blood. He was on his knees and he could not remember how he got there. This nightmare had invaded his bedroom and was arrayed around him. Both men had knives in their hands.

"At the hotel," he said. "At the hotel."

"What hotel? What is her name?"

"Rita Macklin," Funo said.

"What hotel?"

"The Holiday Inn on the beach."

"Does she have the machine?"

"She's a journalist, only a journalist, I'm a journalist—"

"You are a traitor and a thief," Ito said. He looked at the other man, Takahashi. He nodded.

Slash.

The cut was from ear to ear. Funo, again, scarcely felt the edge of the knife because it was so sharp. But he felt blood gurgle in his throat and he realized this was the way his short life was going to end, with a betrayal and with him on his knees, naked at the side of his bed. He wanted to believe this was only a nightmare and that he would wake up in time to live, but now the blood was filling his throat and coming into his mouth and across his lips and he was dying, really dying.

At that moment, Rita Macklin sat very stiff and still in a chair in the terminal of Honolulu International with a large manila envelope on her lap. She wore gray slacks and a gray sweater and she carried no other bag except her purse. The captain had specified speed and she had believed him.

It was a different Captain Peterson sitting in the seat next to her. He had come up and dropped the package on her lap and sat down. He had done all the talking. The talk was almost a whisper and it was very frightened. Peterson's weathered face was not pale but his hands trembled.

"I know you're in a game of your own, you're no more a journalist than I am," he had said over the phone.

"All right," she had replied.

"I knew it. You're the G, aren't you?"

"Am I?"

"Stop fucking me around, I got no time. There's killing going on. People are getting killed and I don't want no part of it. I got the package and I'll turn it over—that's what you want, isn't it? Only I am not goin' to prison for no murders. I don't murder people. I don't want to get killed. What do you say?"

"I say I want to see the package."

"I'll get you the fucking package but I got to go clear. What do you say to that?"

She had waited a moment before answering. "I say, get me the package. Bring it to the hotel."

"I ain't going near no hotel. There's three guys they've killed since I landed last night and they crawled all over the *Pequod*, I missed them by twenty minutes, and when I call the man, the man in Santa Barbara, he hears your name and he freezes but he pretends he doesn't. I don't want no more part of this."

"Denisov," she had said, very softly, building a house of cards and being amazed how high it was.

"I don't know no Denisov."

"The Russian man in Santa Barbara," she had said with more confidence. It had to fit that way; Devereaux had said that name on the morning he came back to Bethesda.

"I know the Russian. His name is Dennis. Mr. Dennis. He could be maybe named that from some Russian name but I don't know no Denisovitch or whatever you said. But you know, don't you? You're ahead of me, aren't you?"

No, she had thought. I know so little. And she had wished Devereaux was there and she could ask him what to do next.

They agreed to meet right away at the airport, Peterson was going to get a flight out for anyplace, he would give her the damned package and she would make promises for the government.

Peterson was whispering, leaning toward her ear like a penitent telling sins. "The city is spooked. Japanese from Tokyo are all over the town and they're not taking any names or prisoners. They sliced Jimmy Wong at midnight, Jimmy was one of my customers. They crawled all over my boat after I left, I got that from one of the boys on the waterfront. Shit, these guys are killers and that's what they want, honey, that little thing on your lap."

"What is it?"

"Exactly what you thought it was."

She stared at the thing as though it might bite her. She was afraid because Peterson was afraid, but she was also excited. It was the thing Devereaux had been after; it was enough to satisfy whoever wanted it from Devereaux, and Devereaux would be freed from his task. That's what she was thinking.

"I want to open it."

"Do whatever you want, I gave it to you. I held up my end, you gotta hold up your end," Peterson said.

"What are you going to do?"

"I'm going to get the hell out of here. I can't leave the *Pequod*, I thought about it, I was going to fly out of here but what the hell am I going to do without my boat? I'm going to take her out until this blows over . . ."

"But you trust me?"

"I don't trust you, I don't trust nobody. But I don't want that fucking package on my hands. You work for the G, I could see that with all the questions you were asking, so you take care of it, you take this damned thing back to them and you leave me out of this. That's the deal. I'm shook, I admit it, but I didn't have nothing to do with no murders and I don't want nothing to do with the fucking Jap gangsters. They're killing people, Miss Macklin, you ought to do something about that."

"Do something about what?"

"Killing people. Taxpayers pay people like you to take care of things like this," Peterson said.

She turned and stared at him. She made her face calm, the way she thought a federal agent would look at him. "We're not interested in you, Peterson. We were interested in the package."

"I know that. You're a spy, aren't you? I thought that's what this was about when that Russian first come to me and talked about taking a package for him. That was months ago. A Russian spy. I hope you put him away for the rest of his life. I didn't know this was something against the government."

"You didn't," she said.

"I swear to God. I don't want trouble with the G. There was only that one time." He was still trembling and he looked around when he talked, though no one was near them.

"All right," she said. Indifferently. She could scarcely contain her excitement but the calm mask across her eyes didn't crack. "You take off. But don't mention my name, not to Denisov or anyone."

"I won't mention your name and don't mention mine," Peterson said. "There wasn't that much money anyway."

In fact, Peterson lied without meaning to.

He mentioned her name once more an hour later as the sun gilded Diamond Head above Waikiki Beach and moved slowly above the horizon. She was aboard the American Airlines flight for Los Angeles, the first of the day, and the package was in her lap still but now she had opened it and seen what it was.

Peterson mentioned her name to two Japanese men named Ito and Takahashi and he had told them she was a government agent and he had told them about Mr. Dennis and an address he had been given on De La Vina in Santa Barbara. He wanted to convince them that he would tell them everything he knew because they had begun the conversation by slicing off his little finger on his left hand. When Peterson had told Ito and Takahashi everything he knew, they ended his life exactly in the way they had ended the life of Ernest Funo. They were close, very close to the trail and the machine was somewhere just ahead of them. They decided to stake out the Holiday Inn where Rita Macklin was expected to be in her room. They would find a way to uncover her and without causing undue attention to themselves. They were sure of that.

TWENTY-ONE

2 Oct 90—SANTA BARBARA

Devereaux opened the door of his hotel room and saw Kevin sitting in the upholstered straight chair. He entered the room and Mickey Connors was in a second chair between the two double beds, reading a book by the nightstand lamp. He folded the book against the spine and laid it on his lap and smiled at Devereaux.

"Kevin and I decided to see how you were making out. Keeping late hours."

"So are you," Devereaux said. He looked at the two men and then turned to the bathroom door. Kevin stood up then but Mickey waved him down.

"Use the facility," Devereaux said.

Went into the room and shut the door. Opened the toilet. Flushed the toilet. He thought about it. Mickey Connors must have a sixth sense about things. Or maybe Langley had told him something that Devereaux didn't know. It was all coming together somehow, he could sense it. Denisov was waiting for the package like an expectant mother who was past due.

He turned on the water faucets and washed his hands and dried them on a towel. Whatever it was, he would have to play it out. And carefully.

He opened the bathroom door and stepped back into the bedroom. He sat down on the edge of the bed. He waited.

The morning light filtered through the shades of the windows.

"We come from New York to talk to you, lad," Mickey Connors said. "Langley don't trust you and don't think we should trust you either."

"I see," Devereaux said. "Was this a new thing with Langley? I mean, did you just decide to run a credit check after you already hired me?"

"Not exactly. Maybe I never did trust you but I wanted to see you in action. Maybe I wanted to see how it played," Mickey Connors said.

"Why don't I tell you the truth?"

Mickey Connors smiled at Kevin. "You mean you might have been holding out on me?"

"I might have been," Devereaux said.

"I told you not to steal and not to lie."

"Maybe holding out isn't the same thing."

Kevin stared at Devereaux with the neutral gaze of a man who can kill very easily. It was the face of a butcher.

"What's the truth of things, fella?" Mickey Connors said. "You might not want to leave anything out now."

"I might not," Devereaux said. "First, the man you don't like in Section. I don't like him either."

"I take it that part was true from the beginning. Your clout was always Hanley. I could see you not getting on with the smoke."

"But he dragged me into this," Devereaux said. Staring at

Mickey now, ignoring Kevin's gaze. Mickey had to understand this, how carefully he had to understand.

"He's got a little blackmail on me. It involves something that has nothing to do with this business. If I can do what he wants, he can cancel the blackmail. Well, I needed time to think it out because if he uses blackmail once, he can always use it again."

"That's the way it works," Mickey Connors said.

"He wanted me to infiltrate your organization," Devereaux said.

"That's why Langley told me not to trust you. But you were on disability. You moved out on your girlfriend. She did a number on you that night you called her from the pay phone in the Croydon. It must be some helluva blackmail."

"It's good enough," Devereaux said. "The point is, what can you do for me?"

"That's pretty rich, fella. You just said you were spying on me."

"Pendleton doesn't know anything yet. About anything. I don't really care if he ever knows. The point is, what can you do for me?"

Mickey Connors pursed his lips and steepled his fingers. He tapped his lips with his fingertips. "You got a bold streak, fella. Why don't you go on and give me an incentive."

"He wants to know about you and everything you do and who works for you. He says he wants to turn you into a supplier and middleman for R Section. I don't believe him. I think he wants to destroy you and let me be destroyed along with it."

"Would he do that?"

"He would do anything. Fifteen years ago, he was in on a little assignment I had in Europe. I was supposed to take an East German agent named Heinemann to the West. It was a setup. This Heinemann nearly killed me and I made

151

an error. A very bad one. I killed two Mossad agents by mistake. When it was all over, I was demoted down to Chad. And Pendleton, who might normally be expected to hold the bag on it, got a promotion for rounding up a Soviet spy ring in the West. I never quite believed in that. I never trusted Pendleton. I still don't. I'm experiencing déjà vu and I want to get out of the trap."

"Why is that?"

"Mickey, I can't get to Pendleton at all. The problem is with the blackmail. If I tell you the blackmail, then you've got it over me too. I've got to have the blackmail destroyed."

"And what about Pendleton?"

Devereaux stared at the man. Mickey's eyes were mild behind the rimless glasses. The prayerful hands unfolded. "Kevin, take a walk. I want to talk to this fella alone."

Kevin got up. "You want a piece?"

"I don't need a piece, do I, Devereaux?"

Devereaux shook his head but kept his eyes on Mickey. Kevin closed the door behind him.

"The point is," Mickey said. "If I do for you, what can you do for me?"

"That's the point," Devereaux said.

"Tell me."

"I can get you the code machine, first of all. The price is supposed to be fifteen million."

"It exists then, it really does?" Mickey couldn't help the enthusiasm that suddenly colored his voice. The rumor of a year's time, heard in a dozen places, was really true.

"The price is supposed to be fifteen million," Devereaux said. "Your Langley reports were right about Denisov. He's waiting for it."

"How do you know?"

"I just came from talking to him."

"Why'd you do that?"

"Because you expected it," Devereaux said. His gray eyes

stared with the vacant intensity of a timberwolf watching its prey.

Mickey Connors got up. It was too much. Nervous energy led him to the window. He looked out at the murky waters off the beach. "Let's get out of here. I can't sit in a room right now, I want to stretch out. Let's take a ride along the beach and see where the road goes."

Devereaux led the way to the lobby and across to the entrance. It was cooler; the wind had shifted to the west and the wind carried the smell and feel of the water.

The rental Cadillac was not a limousine. Mickey said, "You drive."

"Don't you drive?"

"I never learned," Mickey said.

Devereaux smiled. "You weren't interested."

"Driving was never gonna make me a dime. A smart Irishman knows his pleasures and knows what's for fun and what's for money. Driving don't seem much fun to me."

Devereaux got behind the wheel. Mickey settled in the passenger seat.

They went east along Cabrillo Boulevard on the road toward Carpenteria. The traffic was very light; it was too early for anything.

"You want me to ace the smoke for you," Mickey Connors said. "That's a very big favor."

"You can get the machine for nothing," Devereaux said.

"You gonna kill Denisov?"

"It's more complicated than that. This is a setup, Mickey, a setup against me and you. Pendleton again."

"Your favorite blackfella," Mickey Connors said.

"Pendleton was in Zurich a long time ago. Just in time to take me to the hospital. I wondered about that for a long time, the head of Paris desk suddenly appearing in Zurich after a botched job he set me up in. He puts me out there to distract you. That's got to be it. He isn't going to deal with you, Mickey, and if it takes my life to stop you from getting the machine, well, that's an acceptable loss."

"A nice fella," Mickey said.

Devereaux decided. It was an act of betrayal of Section. It was outside all the rules of the game.

"I saw the middle man. Mr. Outside. The man dealing with Denisov."

Mickey caught his breath. He stared at the man with gray eyes and tried to see the truth in them.

"Why would you tell me?"

"Too much coincidence. Denisov to begin with. Denisov and I fought our good fights a long time ago. And now I saw the face of the middle man."

"Who is it?"

"An ex-Stasi. A terrorist named Kurt Heinemann. The man I was sent to get out of Zurich a long time ago. Except I got shot and he got away and there was Pendleton on the scene."

"I don't know about Zurich—"

"You don't have to. This is a trap, Mickey, some kind of fucking trap and I'm swimming right in it like fifteen years ago. Déjà vu. I don't like any of it."

"Why are you telling me?"

"To have a witness. In case I go down. How did Kurt Heinemann get inside Consortium International? Langley doesn't know about him and Langley is backing off this in any case because Denisov was the spy turned by Section—not Langley. Denisov is getting a code machine. He thinks he's dealing with Langley through Consortium."

Mickey understood then. "He's really dealing with R Section."

"And you're in the cold, Mickey. And so am I." There was mist on the pavement, clinging like spider webs to trees and bushes on the roadside. "I called Hanley."

"Hanley."

"You know, my old clout inside Section. Pushed aside by Pendleton. I ran Kurt Heinemann's name past him. Nothing in our files. This is Pendleton's private stash and Kurt Heinemann is his secret. It has to be."

The mist became rain, light and flickering.

The wipers clicked back and forth, keeping time for the separate thoughts of the men in the car.

"You're stepping outside the rules, Devereaux, aren't you?"

"Pendleton started it. He's out of bounds, out of control. He's trying to blackmail me into getting to you, getting to Langley, making you lose the machine and making you dirty to Langley. I want you to take care of it for me, Mickey. And I'll get you the machine."

Silence.

"What about it?" Devereaux finally said.

"We're talking killing here?"

"You know what we're talking about," Devereaux said. He stared straight ahead.

"You're a bastard, right down deep, isn't that right?"

Devereaux said nothing.

"What's the blackmail?" Mickey asked again.

"You'll do it."

"Something will be done."

"I don't think you've got a lot of time. When I get the machine away from Denisov, you'll have to have the other thing done."

"It won't cost me a dime?"

"Not a dime. It's going to cost Consortium International. That ought to make you happy."

Mickey Connors grinned. "Happy as a pig in shit."

Then turned the smile down a bit. "But the blackmail, you're gonna have to tell me that, tell me what I have to find."

"You don't have to find a thing," Devereaux said. "It's

something that Pendleton put together. A lot of things are known but he put the things together in a way that can cause a problem. And Pendleton will be willing to cause that problem. So Pendleton is my problem."

"You had this in mind from the beginning, boy?"

"I had nothing in mind. I was in shock and I needed to think it out. I had to go along with Pendleton and I went to the West Side to see if you'd believe that I was looking for a new trade."

"I could use you for sure," Mickey Connors said. "It ain't often you get a chance to talk to someone as smart as yourself."

"I have to be here and Pendleton can be two thousand miles away. I gave Hanley my telephone number. There's going to be plenty of witnesses that I was nowhere near Pendleton."

"You want a lot from me," Mickey Connors said once more.

"I can give you a lot," Devereaux said.

TWENTY-TWO

Hanley sat in his office. It had a window, unlike his old office when he was chief of Operations. Now he was senior adviser to the director of R Section, Lydia Neumann. The post was as meaningless as the view. He had always been her adviser but Pendleton's takeover of Operations had been a blow to both of them. Lydia Neumann felt out of touch with the way things were going in Section, in the field, at the dozens of stations around the world. Pendleton did not consult with her except as he was formally required to do.

Hanley looked at the telephone number on the slip of paper again. It had been in his pocket for two days. What was Devereaux doing again? Hanley had checked his 201 file. He was still on disability; he was retired from active duty. What was he doing now that involved a German Stasi

157

officer who probably was home safe in Moscow now that the GDR had ceased to exist?

The telephone number of a hotel in Santa Barbara.

Hanley folded the paper again and put it in his wallet. He had been in Section from the beginning, in the Kennedy administration, and he had never felt so alienated in his life. Pendleton expected him to retire, to face down the barrage of boredom and meekly submit his recommendation. Pendleton was clever, very clever, and crude beyond belief in the exercise of power. His subtlety was in knowing when brute pressure would work just as well as finesse.

The light on the phone winked. The phone made a sound.

He picked up the phone and placed it on the doublescrambler and picked up a second receiver.

"Yes."

"November," said the operator inside the classified switchboard on the next floor.

"Put him through."

"Her," said the operator.

The line was switched.

Her?

"November," the female voice said.

"Who is this?"

"Hanley? Rita Macklin."

"You have no access to a code name—"

"I'm in Los Angeles. I have to get in touch with him and I don't know anything, any address or phone—"

"Miss Macklin, I am not your matchmaking service. This is—"

"I know what he's doing, not where. He told me about Denisov. I have the thing. I actually have the thing."

"I don't know what you're saying—"

"A sailor in Hawaii named Peterson was the link. Devereaux had the name because Connors told him."

Hanley pursed his lips in a priggish way. This woman was

a journalist and he had an instinct about journalists that he thought was usually right. And she was the woman who lived with Devereaux. Why didn't she know where Devereaux was?

"I can't tell you anything, Miss Macklin."

"I need to know where Denisov is. Somewhere in Santa Barbara County, I know that. I have a package and an address but maybe it's not the right place. Or maybe I shouldn't deliver it. I don't know. I know that there's violence connected with it. Murder."

"Call the police then, Miss Macklin."

"I want to—"

"No, Miss Macklin."

Silence. The slight buzz of the doublescrambler danced on the line like an echo. "Mr. Hanley," she began.

Hanley said nothing.

"I don't want to call Pendleton. He's . . . working for Pendleton against his will. I don't understand everything but he doesn't trust Pendleton and Pendleton has some terrible hold over him. Maybe he can break it with this package."

"What is the package?"

"The code machine. The Japanese code machine."

Hanley blinked. Of course he didn't know. Pendleton had a very small loop. Sometimes the loop was no bigger than himself. He never advised Mrs. Neumann about anything of substance.

What was Hanley defending except his own ignorance of what was going on around him? He took out his wallet and unfolded the slip of paper.

"He gave me a number," Hanley said. "I trust your discretion. This is not a matter of journalism."

"Do you think I'd hurt him with a story?" she said.

"This is a matter I know nothing about."

"But you have Denisov's address?"

"I have a telephone number."

"For Denisov."

"For the man you choose to live with."

He recited the number slowly and only once.

"Where is he?"

"In a hotel in Santa Barbara," Hanley said, amazed as she was. Hanley felt the perfect frustration of the outsider caught inside a company that has shunned him.

And felt a little of the outsider's retaliation: anger and a sense of hitting back. He was breaking his own rules and he didn't care in that moment.

Devereaux stretched on the bed, his eyes open, staring at the ceiling. Mickey Connors and the ox named Kevin were gone. He thought about them and about Pendleton. The last thing he would have thought about in that moment was the person who called.

He reached for the telephone on the nightstand and picked it up. He didn't utter a word. And then he heard her voice.

She was very good. She gave a fill exactly in the way that it had to be given. She started with the trip to Honolulu to work on phony stories and to find out what she could about a man named Peterson. She told him about Ernie Funo, whom she was unable to raise on the phone. She told him about Peterson and about the machine. And she told him that Peterson had mistaken her for some kind of spy and that Peterson was afraid of Japanese gangsters on his trail.

When she was finished, there was such a long pause that she asked if he was still there.

"Where are you exactly?" he said.

"I'm exactly in the terminal at LAX," she said.

"You're in terrible danger," he said.

"I can handle it."

"You can't handle it. No one can. If the Japanese are this close to recovering the machine, they'll be on a feeding frenzy."

"I'll come to Santa Barbara—"

"Don't think about it. Get the first commuter flight you can out of there. And keep going. I'll meet you at Santa Maria Airport. It's about fifty miles north of here. Just don't fly into Santa Barbara. And get a wig."

"A wig?"

"A wig, a wig. Get something to cover your hair. They'll have Peterson by now. They've got your name and description. Buy a ticket for cash and give them a phony name and get a wig when you can."

"This is silly," she said.

"This is as bad as when they almost caught up with you after Florida. You shouldn't have gotten involved."

"I got the machine. I got the goddamned machine," she said. "You sound like I did something wrong."

But he couldn't tell her how wrong everything was turning.

TWENTY-THREE

In the beginning of the deal, Gandolph had expected to pay in cash but Denisov was too smart for that. He could deal with Kurt Heinemann but it would be on electronic terms. He did not accept cash, only a bank transfer. So Gandolph had arranged to put fifteen million dollars in the account of a certain bank in Zurich with offices on the Paradplatz. Tomorrow, when Heinemann met Denisov, the money would be transferred by Heinemann's telephone call to the Swiss city.

"What do you think?" Gandolph said. He was dressed casually, as casually as a man handing over the key to fifteen million dollars can be under the circumstances. Money changing is always a nervous moment. Not that he didn't trust Kurt Heinemann. When it came down to it, Kurt needed Gandolph—his contacts and protections—more than Gandolph needed him.

They were sitting in the living room of his house in Evergreen in the Front Range of the mountains above the western edge of Denver. The kids and the wife were in Phoenix for the week.

Kurt Heinemann looked down at the cup on the coffee table between them. It was a nice, big house on the hillside, surrounded by trees and privacy. The mountains were clothed in bright colors because of the intensity of the sunlight. They met this way because Gandolph was the only person inside Consortium International who dealt with Mr. Dodge. It had been this way from the moment he was hired. Consortium International had its public meetings but each partner reported in general terms, never in specifics. That way, all their secrets were kept safe and risks were not shared. They liked it that way. Thus, the risk of Miss Browning was slight but real, shared only by Gandolph and, possibly, Mr. Dodge, and Gandolph had taken care of it in a secret way.

What did not occur to Gandolph this bright afternoon was that private risk did not minimize risk at all but, in some cases, exaggerated it.

Kurt Heinemann went to the wall of windows that led to the balcony. He had left the money transfer instructions on the coffee table. He carried a cup of coffee in his hand. He might have gone to the deck to look at the view. It was very nice and very private. The deck was at least a hundred feet above the next bit of ground. Ten stories.

Gandolph joined him on the deck. He shared the view as the owner of it.

"Tomorrow night," Gandolph said.

"*Ja*, tomorrow it will be done."

"When will I see you?"

"I will call you at the house from the airport. I can transfer the machine here."

"Then what?"

"I will take a holiday. Maybe I will go to Mexico. I have never been there."

"Don't drink the water." Another smile.

"So." He put the cup down on a ledge that surrounded the deck. Gandolph smiled at him curiously and inclined his head.

Kurt Heinemann had killed or helped kill many dozens in his years in the Stasi. He saw murder as an instrument of war. Wars were declared and undeclared but killing was only an instrument. In any war, there are innocents. There had been no innocents here except for Mr. Gandolph's wife and his two small children. It had pleased Kurt that they were not in this house and that they would not present a problem.

"So, Mr. Gandolph, we must say good-bye then."

"Good-bye? I told you, we have a lot of opportunities coming up and they're in your line."

"I sold you on the existence of a machine that you yourself had heard existed from contacts with CIA. So, I could get you such a machine."

"Yes."

"Then our business is concluded," Kurt Heinemann said. *"Auf wiedersehen, Herr Direktor."*

"I don't get it."

Kurt plucked the cup of coffee from Gandolph's hand. He placed it next to his own on the deck ledge. Gandolph's smile was definitely descending into a puzzled stare.

"I don't get it," Gandolph said again.

"Because you do not have to get it," Kurt Heinemann said. Black eyes turned cold, face pale in the sunlight, the white scar livid under the eye. Gandolph stepped forward and grabbed at the ledge like a man holding on.

It was the wrong position to take.

Kurt knelt quickly and simply picked him up by the ankles and shoved.

He scarcely had time to scream as he flailed his arms like a high-diver and crashed headfirst on the floor of the forest.

Kurt stared down at the body.

He picked up his coffee and sipped. He kept staring at the body.

He had taken the irrevocable first step away from Pendleton and his servitude in America. He had fifteen million dollars. Tomorrow he would have Ruth with him on a plane to Germany and he would have both fifteen million in his own Zurich account and a machine to generate more money. Whatever happened, he would be back in his own world, fighting the war as the good soldier.

TWENTY-FOUR

2 Oct 90—SANTA BARBARA

Ito and Takahashi were puzzled.

The address that Peterson had given them for Mr. Dennis was a frame dwelling on a slightly gone-to-seed street that contained four apartments.

For a time, they sat in the rental Dodge and debated it with each other in low, harsh voices. It was still daylight and they both felt it, that this was the wrong place. But when a man like Peterson has been disembowled and is trying to save his life by telling the truth, then he tells the truth.

They decided by their sudden lapse into silence.

They entered the apartment on the first floor rented to "Mr. Dennis" but it was absolutely bare.

They decided it was a post office and that the machine would be brought here by the white woman named Rita Macklin.

They had concluded that Rita Macklin had not checked out of her hotel room in Honolulu but had flown to Los Angeles after taking the machine from the unfortunate Captain Peterson, who had died on his knees, cursing them as his own blood filled his mouth.

She had even used her own name on the ticket and purchased it with a credit card. It was hard to believe she was such an amateur.

But why had she not appeared here? And who was Mr. Dennis who directed these labors, first from the sabotage of the *Fujitsu* and the bribery of the unfortunate *Fujitsu* captain to the chicanery of Ernest Funo and Captain Peterson and Rita Macklin?

One of them would sit and wait and the other would find a hotel room and take a little sleep. They had been awake for two days across half a world. There were at least six other teams in other places seeing to other details.

The hijacking of the *Fujitsu* and the loss of the code machine had deeply shamed the organization they belonged to.

Ito and Takahashi did not think of themselves as killers or security agents but as middle management in a large company with good benefits and unlimited possibilities. That their company was a Japanese crime gang and that they had been hired by Masatata Heavy Industries precisely for their skills in the underworld was not material.

"You have to telephone this information to Tokyo," Takahashi said to Ito before they parted.

"Let us resolve some of it first," Ito said in his precise way.

He was smaller and more modern than Takahashi, who was quite a giant by Japanese standards and who practiced the ancient rites of the warrior class he was descended from. Or claimed to be descended from.

Ito said, "It would be to our credit and the credit of the organization to have the machine recovered and the guilty punished in a satisfactory way."

Takahashi deferred. He worked well with Ito because Ito was politically cunning and could judge better the moment when to make this move or that. They had advanced well in harness through the ranks of the crime family.

It was very late in the afternoon and the sun was setting below the Santa Ynez Mountains that stretch all the way to Lompoc in the west.

The setting sun might have made him sleepy standing in the bare room in the bare apartment but Takahashi took the pride of a warrior in his endurance of all manner of deprivation. He had not eaten for a day and said nothing about it to Ito. Even on the flight from Hawaii, he had refused any sustenance except water. It was the purifying way.

At six precisely, a key in the door turned and it opened and Takahashi was ready in the darkness, his knife in hand.

But it wasn't the white woman at all. The light flicked on overhead and a middle-aged man with the body of a bear and mild saintly eyes stared at him and the knife.

It was Mr. Dennis, Takahashi realized, and took a step.

Whatever Denisov realized was not important. He had pulled out the gun quickly and aimed it right at the large Japanese's chest.

Takahashi froze.

"Who are you please?"

Mild. But the gun didn't waver.

"You have stolen our machine."

Denisov stared at him. "Put down the knife," Denisov said.

"I must do what I have to do," Takahashi said and took another step. In a moment, he could spring and kick the pistol out of the small man's hands and begin to ask him questions.

Denisov never contemplated that.

He fired and the pistol sound was very loud in the bare room. The large man in dark suit and hat and white shirt tried to stare cross-eyed at the bullet hole between his eyes. He was actually dead in that moment but the nerves tingled on and he took another step before he was on his knees and then on the floor, kicking in the final agony of existence, the knife still held in his right hand.

TWENTY-FIVE

He waited for her for two hours at the airport, meeting every plane. He pictured her in mind but he picked through the faces of arriving passengers and she never fit the picture. And then she was there, her face haunted with that peculiar weariness all air travelers eventually carry as proof of their flights, no matter how pleasant. But he was still startled to see her, the face of his lover picked out in a crowd of strangers. Their intimate past only heightened the meeting in a drab airport in the company of indifferent strangers.

She had thought to carry the package in a cheap suitcase she bought at the airport in Los Angeles.

She had covered her head with a babushka and wore sunglasses and a T-shirt that said she was a Beach Boys baby.

It was a pretty good disguise because Devereaux had really frightened her. That and calling Funo again and getting the

171

voice of a policeman who wanted to know who the hell she was. That was when she thought Ernie Funo was dead and somehow it was her fault for involving him in this bad business.

They did not kiss or speak to each other. They shared their common weariness in that moment. He took the bag from her and led her out of the airport to his car.

When they got in the car, they kissed for a long moment, hungry for each other as they always were after any separation. But now the strain of everything seemed to make the need for comfort that much greater.

"Will you always rescue me?" she said finally, her lips apart, her eyes closed behind her sunglasses, thinking of him making love to her and wishing they were together in some dark place where it could happen right now. "I always need it."

"You made it simpler. You have the machine. Now I just need the bodies."

The word chilled her. She shivered in the heat of the closed car.

"Are you all right?" he said.

"Nothing," she said. She looked out the side window. "I think Ernest Funo is dead. I called again before I left L.A. and a policeman answered the phone."

"Everyone is going to be dead who was in on taking the machine. And a few along the trail. They're not playing. I just hope they give me enough time to pull it off."

"What are you going to do?"

"Give the machine back to Denisov."

She blinked. She took off her sunglasses. He started the motor and a sweet chill wave of cool air came from the dash. The sun had set quickly behind Santa Maria. She said nothing until they were on Highway 101 back down toward Santa Barbara.

"Why?" she said. "Why give it to him? He put you in this mess from the beginning."

"He was working a deal. It had nothing to do with me."

"Yes it did."

"It's his trail. Because he was the man who stole it. From setting up the plans on the *Fujitsu* all the way through. Because someone has to hold the bag on this. Just so I can open the bag again later."

"What's going to happen?"

"A German named Kurt Heinemann is going to buy the machine. He's an ex-Stasi and a terrorist and he tried to kill me once and almost pulled it off. And he's working somehow for a man who can control him the same way he controls me."

"Pendleton."

"Pendleton. Kurt and his sister, the well-known whore, the three of them," Devereaux said. The words were personal and there was an edge to the way he said them that he rarely used. Devereaux had been cold, distant, gray with contempt once, and he had isolated himself and his emotions from the world he practiced his trade in. Rita had been able to give him love but the coldness remained when Devereaux was in the trade. Now this was something else. She saw it and it frightened her because Devereaux angry was even more terrible than Devereaux as the detached agent of a shadow business.

They pulled off the highway at Solvang because she was asleep and he saw how tired she had become.

The town was as small as a crossroads twenty years ago with Danish settlers and a bakery. Now it had marketed its Danishness into a grotesque collection of vaguely European buildings that housed hotels, restaurants, and curio shops, as unlike any place in Denmark as it was any place in California.

He booked a room in a quiet hotel and she went up to take a shower. He used a pay telephone in the lobby.

The telephone rang for a long time and when Denisov came on the line, he said, "What?"

"Mr. Dennis. I have a package that belongs to you."

Silence.

"What do you expect me to say?"

"I expect you to say thank you," Devereaux said.

"What do you want?"

"I don't want the money or the code machine. I want Kurt Heinemann and that loony sister."

Silence again.

"That can be arranged. But why do I trust you?"

"Because I have an honest face. Because I have the machine."

"There is a dead Japanese in the building on De La Vina."

"Good. Just one? There's more than one."

"I have . . . a business acquaintance in the house. If there are more, they will be . . . taken care of."

"And where is the crazy woman?"

"Gone to signal her brother. The money is set, all is set. Except I don't have the machine."

"You know he's going to kill you."

"I expect that he thinks he will. I am careful, Devereaux, you know that. This is a bank transfer."

"He's going to kill you and steal your money and the machine."

"He is involved with . . . a very large middle firm that will sell the machine to CIA. Why would he kill me?"

"For fifteen million and a machine he can use to generate more money. He's going to double-cross you and CI both. Kurt Heinemann disappeared last year when the wall came down and Section thinks he disappeared to Moscow. Section is wrong. And one person in Section knows it."

"Perhaps," Denisov said.

"Time to bet, Denisov. On him or me. But I have the machine."

"What do you want so badly that you give it to me?"

"I want Kurt Heinemann. I don't really want his sister but I might have to take her anyway, she's a loose cannon looking to go off in the wrong place."

"She is an exquisite lover."

"With fifteen million, you can buy a world of experience."

"Perhaps," Denisov said.

Another silence, exactly like the periods of inaction between chess moves.

"Who do you work for?"

"A man named Mickey Connors."

"A second group. They will take the machine."

"They will take the machine and allow you fifteen million of Consortium International money. A nice trade for them. And all I need is Kurt Heinemann to make it stand up. Kurt will disappear and all the Japanese gangsters and spies in the world won't be able to bring him back."

"You can do this?"

"You know," Devereaux said.

"At three P.M. We meet first on Cabrillo. Do you know the bench across from the large hotel?"

"I know the bench."

"We will meet and talk and transfer his funds. And then I will give him the code machine."

"And he will kill you."

"We will be in a public place. I will have the sister with me in the car. Believe me, I will have a hostage."

"So he'll follow you. You have to release her."

"There might be a second car. Or a third. Getting away is easier if he must be distracted by the peril to his sister."

"What peril?"

"I cannot say at the moment."

"All right. You can have the machine," Devereaux said.

"And don't double-cross me. There are more people than me in this."

"I know the name of the Irish in New York. But he did not approach me in the beginning."

"Because he didn't know how to do it," Devereaux said. "The machine will be there at the right time."

"When?"

"At the right time," Devereaux said. He replaced the receiver. He thought about it and then dialed the number in New York.

"Dougherty's."

"Tell Mick there's a new number in California and to call it now."

"Do I look like his answering machine?"

Devereaux repeated the number of the hotel in Solvang and hung up. He took the elevator to his room.

Rita was naked in bed under the covers. She was staring at the television set but the sound was muted and she was only staring at the pictures on the screen. It was supposed to help her to see something else but all she could see was Ernie Funo on the screen, in the faces of all the actors. The shock remained and she thought she might never sleep again.

He took a long shower before he joined her beneath the crisp sheets. He held her. For a moment, she could not respond to his holding her. She stared at the television screen full of muted actors.

And then she began to cry.

They talked about it for a long time before they made love. Making love was an overwhelming urge, all the more overwhelming because of the shared peril. They were in the middle of the act when the telephone rang.

He stopped.

"Jesus," she said, "let it ring."

He picked it up on the third ring.

"Why there, boy?"

"Making an arrangement," Devereaux said. "How does it look from your end?"

"Close."

Devereaux said, "Three tomorrow."

"Jesus." Soft, not a prayer or a curse but an expression of awe. And then silence. "All right, fella. It's so close I'll just have to do it myself. And Devereaux. Kevin's there watching so don't do anything I wouldn't do."

They broke the connection.

He looked at her. She was leaning on her right elbow and her breasts were bared and she had the strange and shivering look she sometimes got before she was satisfied. She stretched out her hand but he couldn't, now he couldn't do it at all. He could not explain he had just made the final arrangement for an assassination of a government official.

TWENTY-SIX

Kurt Heinemann was in a killing mode.

He wore it like a uniform.

His clothes were night dark, his sallow face paler because of his outfit. People did not look at him directly when he looked like this. He frightened them, not for what they knew but because something deep and terrifying had colored his features.

He had taken a United flight from Denver to San Francisco International and then spent over two hours booking a confusing trail.

He and Ruth would be on that trail on the night of the third.

They would fly by private helicopter to SFX from Santa Barbara and from there they would take the Delta flight to Seattle where they would change to an Alaskan Airlines flight to Anchorage. They would spend the night in Anchorage and wait for a Japan Airlines flight through from Tokyo to Frankfurt. He had liked that last touch most of all, using Japan Airlines.

He had checked with the hotel in Santa Barbara and, no, Mr. Dever was not in but he was still registered and would there be a message? No message. Mr. Dever-Devereaux would get the message in the morning just as Kurt Heinemann had delivered it to him in that Zurich whorehouse fifteen years ago.

Pendleton had been useful and Pendleton thought it would be like that day in Zurich with an eye for an eye and a trade for a trade.

But this was very different. He would kill Devereaux for Pendleton and Pendleton would have his alibi about infiltrating the Mickey Connors gang and the death of a spy.

When it was over, Pendleton could convince his business rivals at Langley that Mickey Connors had stolen the machine, but he would not have either the machine or Heinemann.

Pendleton would probably survive in good shape but he would be unable to admit that the German ex-Stasi had worked for him on unofficial staff or that the German had betrayed him. It was a neat box, made with Pendleton's own hand.

Heinemann left the San Francisco airport in a large, fast car from Avis and started south after 10:00 P.M. Highway 101 plunged down the coast through San Jose and Salinas toward the jewel cities of San Luis Obispo and Santa Maria and then down to Santa Barbara. He had the device of his choosing. It was a hotel room bomb that was simple: plastique and a primer set off when a door is opened or a suitcase unzipped.

He also had a Beretta automatic fitted with a silencer. If Devereaux was sleeping in his own bed, he would die; if he had not returned when Heinemann arrived, there would be the booby trap.

In any case, the pistol would be used on Denisov when they transferred the funds. Ruth had assured him two days ago she was leaving Denisov and would not be in the way when the transfer was made. Everything was prepared.

Except that Ruth had not answered the telephone all day from the safe house they had set up in Los Angeles. She might have found someone else to like.

Kurt thought of his mother then and their shared last talk in the dim twilight of that living room in Leipzig with the world crumbling around them.

Ruth, Ruth.

He settled on the bomb because Devereaux was not in his room in Santa Barbara. He called Ruth again at the safe house in Los Angeles and she didn't answer. He fell into a troubled and brief sleep in the few hours before dawn.

TWENTY-SEVEN

3 Oct 90—SANTA BARBARA

Devereaux left her before dawn. They kissed but did not speak at all except to say they loved each other.

He put the package in the trunk of the rental car. He slammed the lid in the darkness and slipped into the driver's seat. The car rattled into life and settled into a slow growl on 101 on the way back to Santa Barbara. The dawn comes late to spots along the coast above the Santa Barbara Channel because of the mountains but you can always see the streaks of light in the water.

He thought about Mickey Connors on the way, thought about the linchpin he was counting on. If Mickey double-crossed him, there was no comeback and he would still have Pendleton and still the threat of blackmail. Then he would have to figure out some way of his own.

He pulled into the courtyard of the large hotel at eight. He needed a shower and he needed to change his clothes. He took the elevator to his floor.

He nearly opened the door all the way. But there had been a time more than a year before when he had carelessly pushed into a hotel room in Washington, D.C., and nearly ended his life because of a bomb blast. Now he was in the habit of opening the door while braced against the wall away from the jamb.

The bomb popped but the force of the explosion was enough to splinter the door into bits of wood, plastic, and pieces of steel. His left hand was cut and the key was destroyed. There wasn't any time for explanations. He went into the room and removed the suitcase and looked around to see if he had forgotten anything. He was out of the room while doors were still opening on the floor and people in nightclothes were standing around, staring at the opening.

He felt better than he had any time since the thing with Pendleton began.

It would be a long day of waiting for everyone.

Denisov in his apartment on Alisos had decided on the solution of tying up Ruth and gagging her. It was not a cruelty he wished to inflict but it was necessary. She had tried to scream and he didn't want to kill her. Well, in any case, he did not want to kill her while he still needed her.

He had packed his baggage in the second car, a Porsche. There were tickets waiting for him in Los Angeles at the airport. He had arranged everything and this was his last morning in America. New passport, new identity; it would work out, all of it.

The business associate watching for Japanese gangsters had telephoned at 12:31 P.M. The phone rang in the bedroom and kitchen. Denisov had decided to sleep on the couch because Ruth Sauer, quite frightened now and much more docile, was tied and gagged in the bed. The "business associate" said the night had been quiet.

"Then there were only two of them," Denisov had said thoughtfully. "You can close the business now and leave the two men in the post office."

"Is there anything else?"

"Send me the bill. I have to go to Los Angeles over the weekend. I'll take care of it when I come back."

A casual conversation, routine business. The second Japanese had shown up at the apartment building shortly before eleven at night and Denisov had a hired gun waiting for him. He had been taken care of in the same way as the first, but with a silencer on the weapon of his hired gun. A thousand dollars was all it had cost Denisov.

Denisov sat at the kitchen table and glanced through the pages of the *Los Angeles Times*. He did not read any story to the end. He noted there was a report in the business section that Masatata Heavy Industries claimed business rivals were suspected of sabotaging the *Fujitsu* and that the Japanese government had promised an investigation. The company named no names. For some reason, the stock had risen seventy-five points on the Tokyo Exchange due to Far Eastern rumors of a company breakthrough in a new product area.

Denisov nodded.

A breakthrough. He felt very calm because he had prepared very well. And even the appearance of Devereaux had not really upset his plans.

At 3:00 P.M., they met on the bench. The ocean smelled fresh and the air was very warm.

Kurt Heinemann said, "You have the machine."

"I have it in a safe place," Denisov said.

"Where is the safe place?"

"In my apartment. Where your sister is."

"Why is my sister in your apartment?"

"I want to show you a photograph. I took it an hour ago."

He took out the Polaroid photograph.

It was Ruth. She was bound and gagged. She stared at the camera and there was a bruise around her left eye. On the table next to her was a device with wires and what appeared to be a fuse linked to putty or clay which had spikes embedded in it.

"This was not necessary," Kurt said, staring at the photograph, feeling anger from the pit of his belly.

"Crudities are necessary. I want you to see. The code machine is in my apartment. You will cross the street to that hotel and make a call that will transfer the money from your account in Zurich to my account. This is the number. And then you will come to my apartment and take the machine."

Simply said. Without any urgency, as though they might sit on this bench and pass the time of day for the rest of the afternoon. Denisov had waited too long and planned too well.

"And what about Ruth?"

"You will take the machine and we will leave together. I have a car and I do not plan to run a race through Santa Barbara. I will have fifteen minutes and you will have to remove the bomb from the table by your sister. You see? It is my precaution. You gave it to me. You let your sister spy on me and she wanted to live with me and you permitted it. You gave me the idea."

"What if I just kill you now?"

"On this public street? In the middle of the afternoon. This is not Moscow. You cannot abduct citizens or kill them as you wish."

"I don't like this at all."

"I like it even less to reach this point of mistrust. But I think we agree to mistrust each other, eh? I don't need the machine but I need that money. You either have it or you don't."

Kurt had envisioned something very different.

Traffic crawled by. The beach was full of sunbathers and strollers, it was that warm today.

"And what if you cross me?"

"Then you know where to get me, eh?"

"How do I know you have it?"

And there was a second Polaroid photograph, this time a picture of a small laptop computer machine propped in front of the chair where Ruth sat tied to a bomb.

"Why are you delaying me?" Denisov said. "There is a trigger on the primer and if Ruth becomes too nervous, she only has four inches of slack. The trigger will set off the bomb. Do you want to do that to your sister?"

"The Russian mentality," Kurt said, sneering the words with contempt. "Crude people."

"It is true," Denisov said.

Silence between them.

"*Ja*, as you say," Kurt suddenly said and got up. He crossed the boulevard carefully, moving in and out of the slow-moving traffic, and Denisov watched him. Then he got up and walked to his small red car, the first car. He drove up the hillside to prepare the place on Alisos for his reception.

Mickey Connors and Kevin watched him pull away and Kevin swung the big car into traffic behind him. "What about the other fella?" Kevin said to his boss.

"I don't give a shit about him. I want the code machine and that monkey Russian must still have it. Kurt Heinemann is Devereaux's problem."

Denisov went into the apartment and, ignoring Ruth, went to the closet, and the Russian took out the oiled rags that held the gun. It was a killing gun, bigger than it had to be. He fitted the silencer onto the barrel and looked at her all the time. She could not see him because he was behind her and she did not dare move.

He stepped into the front room and went to the window again and looked down. There was no one on the sidewalk.

He walked to the kitchen and opened the refrigerator and took out a bottle of milk. He poured the milk into a glass and drank it. Then he put the milk bottle back.

His calm was almost enervating.

He went back to the window and looked down and now he saw Kurt's car swing up the street. He went to the telephone and dialed.

The bank in Zurich provided a twenty-four-hour international service because it was accustomed to odd customers who dealt in odd hours with heavy amounts of money. The Swiss confirmed, in perfect English, that fifteen million dollars had been transferred into his numbered account.

He nodded to the machine and replaced the receiver. It was done. The peace spread throughout his body. It didn't matter about Kurt Heinemann now except that Kurt must be killed.

A body slammed against the front door and splintered it down the middle, the deadbolt holding part of the door.

The shock made the walls tremble.

Denisov picked up the pistol and aimed it at the large young man who was standing with his own pistol in the middle of the room. The two men had never seen each other before this day.

Denisov didn't understand it at all. And Kevin did not understand it either. They stared at each other openmouthed.

"That's two to one, fella," Mickey Connors said behind him. He was half-hidden in the doorway behind the big man. "Kevin'll get you or I will or we'll have a nice sit-down instead and get to know each other."

"What do you want?"

"The machine, Denisov. Did I say your name right?"

"You're Mickey Connors. Devereaux said he worked for you."

"Well, everyone's entitled to stretch the truth now and then. In a way, I suppose he thought he did. He figured we had a deal."

"I don't have the machine," Denisov said.

"Is that a fact?"

"Devereaux got the machine. I don't know how."

"I don't know how—"

"His girlfriend knew everything," Denisov said. "Devereaux must have gotten the machine from her. He called me last night. He said he had the machine. He said he wanted Kurt Heinemann."

Slowly, carefully, Mickey Connors entered the room. He stared at Denisov. "You was gonna sell it to Kurt Heinemann for CI. I was willin' to pay for it. Fifteen million."

"*Da.* I would have sold it but now I'm sold. Devereaux stole my machine."

Mickey Connors grinned at that. "In a manner of speakin', it was your machine. Or anyone else who had his hand on it. The son of a bitch. He was in Solvang and he had the fuckin' machine while he was jobbing me on the phone. He had the machine and she was with him on it." He shook his head. And he shoved his pistol back into his leather coat. "I had him by the balls for a while and let him go. Put the pistol away, Kevin. And you, Denisov. We don't need pistols now."

"But I do," Denisov said. "Stand away from the door. There is someone coming for me and he will not be happy about that I do not have a machine." Only rarely now did the grammar lapse but the wave of calm had passed. The two Irishmen made him nervous now.

"Heinemann?"

Denisov said nothing.

"Look here," Mickey offered, "we can make a deal on the spot. You let me take Heinemann and I can get the machine for myself."

"Why would I do this?"

"For money, why else?"

"How much money?"

Quiet.

"Quickly," Denisov said.

"A hundred grand," Mickey Connors said.

"You don't have that money."

"I can transfer it to you, bank transfer, just pick up a telephone."

"Two hundred thousand," Denisov said.

"Done," Mickey Connors said, and they all three heard the downstairs door and the footsteps on the carpeted stairs.

"Go ahead," Denisov said.

Mickey Connors made a nod and Kevin stepped away from the middle of the room. The stairs rose to the second floor just to the left of the door to the apartment. Mickey Connors stepped to the head of the stairs and pointed his pistol at the top of Kurt Heinemann's head just as he emerged from the stairwell. Kevin was behind and took the pistol from Heinemann's hand. "Inside," Kevin said.

Denisov said, "You transferred my money and now I do not have to kill you because these gentlemen from New York have taken an interest in you."

"This is a double-cross," Kurt said. "I'll kill you. You know I will, Denisov. Tomorrow or the next day, I don't care where you run in Europe."

It was a perfectly reasonable threat coming from a man

who had helped run terror networks through the world for twenty years.

Denisov looked at the older Irishman. "What do you want to do with him?"

"I want to see how much he's worth to Devereaux," Mickey Connors said. "The man with the code machine wanted him more than the machine. Besides, he can't job that machine himself. He needs contacts. And he needs me. I ain't the government; unfortunately, he is."

Kurt turned and kicked the gun away from Kevin so quickly that no one reacted at first.

Mickey Connors reacted with the skill of a street fighter. He struck the German on the back of the head, hard as a cop using a nightstick, without care for the consequences. Kurt dropped to his knees and held out his arms for balance and Mickey hit him again and this time Kurt Heinemann groaned and fell full-length on the rug.

"Close the door, Kevin. Y'aren't hurt, lad?"

"I'm not hurt. He surprised me."

"Happens to the best of them," Mickey Connors said. He smiled at Denisov. "You shoulda shopped with me in the first place, Russian. I know how to make a deal and keep it."

"But Devereaux was part of your deal and now he has the machine. Would you keep it like that?"

"Devereaux is a problem," Mickey said.

Silence. And then Denisov said, "I must leave now."

"Don't you want your money?"

"No, no. You do not intend to give me any money, Mr. Connors. You intend to cheat me. You only want my account and then you would kill me and rob me and still try to get the machine. I am not such a fool as that."

Mickey smiled. "Maybe we'll just work on you anyway and get the account."

Denisov took off his glasses then and put them in a case

in his coat. It was two to one and had been. They both looked like killers who wouldn't flinch at a thing. "How much time do you have? You broke down my door. It is afternoon. Maybe people have called the police already. How much time do you think it would take you to find my account number? You don't even know what city. There is Lichtenstein as well as Geneva. Or Zurich. Or Luxembourg. Or the Bahamas. Would it take you a day? All night? No, you might get it or you might not but you don't have any time. I think I will leave now."

Mickey Connors made a chewing motion and bit his lip. He was frowning now and looked at Kevin, who was made for murder.

"He's right and he's cool enough. All right, Kevin. I hate to see the money go but we can't afford it. California isn't our territory."

Denisov smiled at him. "I thank you now."

"You don't have to thank anyone. You should have dealt with me in the first place," Mickey Connors said. "It's a shame. You know where Devereaux is?"

"I know he has my machine. It is your problem now."

Kevin had murder in his eyes. There was no heat to it, just a cold and even sleepy look that meant killing as a casual act.

Mickey Connors stood aside, straddling the fallen German agent.

"Thank you," Denisov said. He stepped over the body and through the broken doorway. He pulled the door behind him and it would only partially close on the cracked jamb.

"Why'd you let him go?"

"Because Devereaux does have it and I got the thing Devereaux wants. I don't understand all of it but somehow this woman, his little girlfriend, she was working with him hand in glove. The fucking devious bastard, he never trusted me."

"That's right."

Devereaux stood in the bathroom door. The pistol was

small and dark. "I didn't think you were going to let him go, Mickey. That was generous of you. It shows a good instinct."

Slow, surprised. The smile spread across the lean Irish face and lit the eyes.

"You got it, don't you?"

"It's safe, Mickey. You did my deal for me, didn't you?"

"I did. I held my end."

"You fucking liar. I called Pendleton a half hour ago. He's out playing golf."

"That's where it happens, on the golf course."

"He doesn't play golf. He was in his office. You never intended to make an even trade."

Mickey shook his head. "And neither did you."

"On the floor, Kevin, facedown, hands and feet spread."

Kevin got on the floor. He had no doubt about the man with the gun. He had seen him use it on a man he didn't even know in a basement of a warehouse in New York. And he knew that look in the gray eyes, just as cold as his own. He could be made for killing too.

Devereaux watched Mickey's face while he patted Kevin's body and removed the gun. Then he crossed to Mickey Connors and put the pistol against his nose. "Now yours."

"At least you didn't make me get down on the floor."

"My respect for the Kennedys and your father's connection with them."

"You and Rita Macklin cooked this together. You were fucking me over and fucking Pendleton over."

"No. What I told you was true. But you didn't want to do me the favor."

Devereaux stepped back with the piece in his hand and threw the other gun on the desk. "I wanted Kurt Heinemann and you didn't believe me. Greed got in your way."

"You don't kill a government agent like that. It takes time and I didn't have the time to set it up."

193

"But you thought about it," Devereaux said. Sarcasm was squeezed cold.

"I did, I seriously did, but I didn't see how I could do you the favor."

"Kurt had his agenda and you had yours and I had mine and we couldn't seem to get together. I suppose you can't trust people like us," Devereaux said. He wasn't smiling but something made Mickey smile.

"So you're going to shop the machine yourself. To Pendleton. Make your brownie points with the smoke."

"I can't, Mick. I told you that. Pendleton and I are in this too deep. He's broken all the rules and he knows it. More important, Kurt Heinemann knows it. Going back fifteen years."

"Kurt Heinemann? Who you going to give him to? Langley? You think Langley will do you a favor and bust Pendleton for you? You aren't naive, are you, lad? The G takes care of itself. It doesn't go running to tell stories."

"I don't need Langley. I need to settle a debt I picked up once and to settle a score at the same time. The trouble is with you, Mickey, thinking I was so far down that I couldn't see my way up. That's bad character judgment."

"I must of liked you," Mickey Connors said. "I must of believed you."

"You wanted to use me to find a way to get the machine because you said it yourself, Langley couldn't make the approach. And you figured that I was a secondary consideration. Especially after our little heart-to-heart in the car the other morning in the rain. I wanted you to take out Pendleton and you knew I was down to my last resource."

"You figure it that close?"

"That close."

"What if I had taken you up on it and whacked him?"

Devereaux smiled. The smile was the first one on his face.

"Then, Mick, I would have given you the goddamned

code machine," Devereaux said. He crossed to the desk and punched in a local number.

"Time," he said. And replaced the receiver.

"You can't trust Pendleton. You do tricks for him and he'll take you out just as soon as he has the chance."

"He had the chance in Zurich a long time ago. And now, in Santa Barbara. If it hadn't been for Rita deciding to go to Hawaii . . . if it hadn't been for a lot of things, I might have been dead in bed this morning. If you get caught by a blackmailer, you have to find a way to put him in your power. You can't use threats, you have to use other things. I used you and I was lost, I couldn't figure out how you could work for me. But you had to tell me some things and I made a big mistake."

"What was that?"

"I trusted someone. I told someone and it worked out." And he thought of the pain of that moment with Rita Macklin in the apartment in Bethesda when he had let down his guard and confessed some of his trouble to her. Peterson in Hawaii. One name and it had spurred her to save him.

The door opened.

There were three of them, young and nervous in appearance with drawn pistols. One was a woman with dark, darting eyes and a fierce expression on her face. They looked at the two men on the floor and then at Devereaux.

"That's him," Devereaux said. He nodded at the unconscious Kurt Heinemann. "And the woman in the bedroom. She's rigged to a bomb but it's been deactivated."

"We thought only the man—"

"They're brother and sister," Devereaux said. "Inseparable."

Kurt groaned and pushed at the floor and began to rise. One of the men stepped toward him and placed an automatic in his left ear.

He stopped rising.

195

"On the floor," the man said. And Kurt felt his arm kicked out from under him. He hit the floor hard and an involuntary moan escaped him.

"What is this about then?" Mickey Connors said, his hands apart from his coat, looking around the busy room.

But Devereaux didn't have time now.

The woman said, "What about the machine?"

"In the trunk of the red Nissan around the corner. Here's the key," Devereaux said.

The third man led Ruth from the bedroom. Her ordeal showed in her eyes. He had not taken the gag from her mouth. The presence of four guns displayed in such a small space seemed to overwhelm them all with the tension of violence. Even the gun-holding trio were hostage to it and it made their movements sharp, almost violent.

The woman with the pistol slipped it into her pocket and knelt beside Kurt. She produced a roll of duct tape and wrapped it around his mouth.

"Hands behind your back."

Tape again.

She pulled him to his feet roughly by pulling his hair.

Mickey Connors seemed amused by all the activity. "More Section agents than I figured you had the clout to get. You must be on Pendleton's winning team."

"Pendleton is not on mine," Devereaux said. "But this was overdue."

"You didn't get nothing out of it, lad, not a thing. Pendleton double-crossed you and double-crossed you and he'll do it again soon as he gets the chance. You want to tell me about that blackmail?"

"No, I don't think so, Mick. I don't think we have to go into it now."

The three with guns were leading the two Germans out of the room but Devereaux held up his hand. He wanted to see their faces. Ruth glared at him but Kurt was different.

He was the same as he had been that morning in Zurich when he had thanked him for killing the Mossad on his trail.

Fifteen years. Devereaux had thought about it from time to time in the isolated life he had led, even thought about it in nightmares that visited him after he had met Rita Macklin. He had never told her everything though he had explained the scar on his chest with the sort of clinical detail that did not invite closer scrutiny. There had been a lot of people in between but Kurt had been bad enough.

"Mossad," Devereaux said.

And was rewarded by the black, calm eyes going wide.

TWENTY-EIGHT

Cable cars were packed with tourists and ordinary San Franciscans resorted to buses and cabs. The hills were wet with the sort of fog-induced rain that sweeps the sun away from time to time and buries the Golden Gate Bridge in a heavenly gloom. It is a beautiful city because it evokes such a sense of isolation and exile.

They were in the Fairmont Hotel and now they could make love to each other to bury the horror of the past weeks of separation and the trail of murder. The newspapers announced the arrest and detention in Israel of Kurt Heinemann, the ex-Stasi terrorist expert who was linked to any number of terror factions in Europe and the Middle East. The Israeli announcement said he had been apprehended "abroad." And that he was being examined for his role in the 1972 attack on the Israeli Olympic team in Munich. There was no mention made at first of Ruth Sauer.

Rita Macklin smiled at the gift of flowers on the table of the large hotel room and at the candy.

"I feel like my mother must feel on Mother's Day," she said.

"I love you. I never meant to put you in harm's way. I don't know why I told you all those things. I was frustrated that day in Bethesda, I couldn't see any way out of this."

"But now you can."

"It was Pendleton. I couldn't tell you about it then. He had a way to get me to do something for him and I knew it was extracurricular, out of Section, but I couldn't stop him."

"What was it?"

"Two years ago, you went to the Soviet embassy in Washington and the FBI took your picture. You were carrying a large envelope. Five days earlier, the Section took your picture at the consulate in Leningrad. You met with Felix Bloch."

"I went to college with Felix."

"Felix Bloch was arrested a year ago by the FBI but they couldn't prove anything. They thought he was a spy. Felix Bloch gave you an envelope and R Section had the photographs. Put it with the photographs in Washington and they might have had a case, only they didn't put the photographs together. FBI sent over information on you to R Section about the time Pendleton took over Hanley's old job, running operations. Pendleton liked it well enough."

"That was the blackmail? Photographs? I was carrying my pad and tape recorder in that envelope. In Washington. It was raining."

"I don't know anything about Felix Bloch except he was mixed up in something and FBI and Secret Service both know it but don't have enough to prove it without revealing something important. At least, that's my guess. But that wouldn't have stopped Pendleton. He wanted me to be set up and he wanted me to destroy Mickey Connors's organization."

"But that blackmail couldn't work, it—"

"You would have been out of a job for the rest of your life, Rita. Even if it never made it to court. Your magazine wouldn't have kept you on, you know it. And no one would hire you or trust you again. That's all you've got."

"I had you."

"And I would have been the star against you. An agent in R Section living with a journalist who made trips to Russia to see a man under FBI investigation, a man fired from his government job at an important consulate. No. You would have been shopped and I would have shopped you just because I knew you."

"Why didn't you tell me?"

"Because you would have fought it. You would have hired a lawyer or gone to your friend at the *New York Times*. The business would have been murky and you would have gone down. Believe me. I know journalism and I know my own trade. When they want to set you up, they set you up. We do that for a living, Rita."

"Disinformation."

"Worse. We can ruin lives."

Silence on a Sunday morning in a hotel room on top of Nob Hill. The gloom of the city scratched at the windows of the room. She sat in bed, her arms around her knees, staring at the window. He told her these things sitting on the overstuffed chair by the breakfast cart.

"And you can tell me now."

"Now."

"I hate him."

"It doesn't matter. It's over for us."

"Why?"

"Because of Kurt Heinemann. Three days ago, I thought

I saw a way clear but it had to happen quickly. I called a man in Mossad and we met in Solvang. In the same hotel we stayed in. I laid it out for him. He called back in six hours and agreed to it. Then I had to move on the timetable. Denisov was showing signs that the end was coming and Heinemann would get the code machine and I would be left out in the cold again."

"You could have told them Heinemann was in Denver—"

Devereaux shook his head.

"I didn't know where he was. Only Ruth knew. I knew he worked for Consortium International but it might have taken me months to crack it. It's a cooperative of sorts, each unit takes care of itself."

"So you had to wait on the deal. On Denisov."

"It was the easiest way."

She shook her head.

She got up from the bed and went to the window and looked down at the fog and could not see the street below. "And it was my fault. That Ernie Funo was killed."

"It was my fault for telling you anything."

"I feel lost sometimes," she said.

He came up behind her and held her. She wanted that.

"Why is it all right about Pendleton now?"

"Because Kurt Heinemann worked for him. An ex-Stasi terrorist wanted by Israel for more than fifteen years. A terrorist we had twice and twice let go, once in Zurich and once after the collapse of the GDR. Heinemann is going to bring Pendleton down. I called him this morning at home while you were asleep."

"You called Pendleton?"

"I told him to read the morning papers. I told him that Heinemann would tell the Israelis all about his year in America and how he had worked for an American control named Pendleton of R Section. I told him I did it and that I could hold out the information or I could use it."

"You told him that?"

Devereaux smiled behind her. It was a hard, mean smile and it was all right because she didn't see it, did not see the sheer anger behind it.

"He's going to think about it."

"About what?"

"Retirement."

TWENTY-NINE

He often sat alone in his town house off M Street in curious old Georgetown. He had never found the time or inclination for a hobby and now the days were vast and empty and there was this burning in him. Pendleton had been visited twice by the man who was now director of Operations again. The sight of Hanley enraged him as much as anything, as much as Heinemann's secret testimony and an array of documents that proved now that Pendleton had compromised the integrity of R Section for the sake of ambition.

He had broken the Soviet networks in 1976 with information contained that morning on a sheet of paper passed to him in a brothel in Zurich. He had used an agent inside R Section named November to clear the Mossad off the trail of a terror director named the Double Eagle. Kurt Heinemann

205

had told the Israelis everything because he had felt betrayed by Pendleton.

And Pendleton had used his power to threaten the same agent fifteen years later, to use him in illegal espionage inside the United States.

And Pendleton had provided secret bona fides for the German terrorist named Double Eagle and induced him to work within the United States for a shadowy company called Consortium International. Along the way, he had approved the acquisition of a code machine by murder and theft from a prominent company of a friendly power.

Hanley would explain these things to Pendleton with obvious satisfaction and with a certain cold, even prissy, tone of voice.

"Devereaux was outside the law as much as he was in it all the time he worked for you," Pendleton exploded during the second visit.

"You broke the laws, Pendleton, but you did worse. You broke the rules."

"I resigned because of blackmail."

"What blackmail?"

"What are you going to do with this information? The Jews got their terrorist and they got the goddamned machine and they don't even acknowledge there is a machine."

"Not publicly," Hanley had said.

"I could still blow this open."

"You could still spend the rest of your life in prison," Hanley had responded.

The days were very long even as the time of daylight grew shorter.

And one late afternoon, a gray car that might have been a Ford or Chevrolet, or something like that, pulled up to the town house off M Street. The driver waited and Pendleton came down the steps and got into the car. He sat next to the driver and studied his face.

"Why can't Hanley come here?"

"Not this time. He says you insult him," Devereaux said.

"He can arrest me but he can't just keep harassing me."

"He doesn't want to arrest you. You can hurt Section badly with everything you did. It would embarrass a lot of people. Congressional investigations. He doesn't want that."

"He doesn't want that."

"And you." Devereaux stared at him for a moment. "You don't want that either. That brings prison because you misused your office."

"You are one sanctimonious son of a bitch."

"You set me up twice. I took it personally," Devereaux said.

"All because of that bitch."

"Don't ever speak of her."

Pendleton grinned. It might have been his only real hobby, tearing the wings off people and tying cans to their tails. He had nettled Devereaux and that was what passed for a triumph in these empty days of enforced retirement.

They crossed over Key Bridge and took the Beltway south and they were long past downtown and the Mall where R Section was tucked away in the top floor of the Department of Agriculture Building.

The air was heavy with the thought of rain. The colors were still open on the trees in the long, languid autumn of Washington and Virginia and Maryland.

"Where we going?"

"We're using a safe house down in Charles County. Along Indian Head Highway," Devereaux said.

"Why?"

"Because Hanley said he didn't want you to set foot ever again inside Section. He said you soiled it too long to ever go back to it."

"You're all pushing me too much. I might just decide to take a chance and strike back."

"Hanley doesn't want you to harm R Section anymore."

The highway was divided and busy with homebound commuters going to the sprawl of hamlets that led all the way down to Indian Head itself and the Naval Propellant Plant at the end of the road. Some twenty years before, it had been very rural and suspiciously southern but the hunger for housing tracts for commuters to the District had pushed back the forests along the Potomac River and Charles County was no longer the home of slot machines and little farms.

In most parts.

He turned at a highway that led east toward the main highway up the western shore of Chesapeake Bay. But they didn't go that far. There was a turnoff into a woods and the dirt road did not lead far, only far enough for them to see the swamp ahead. It was a bog, ground low and spongy.

Devereaux looked at Pendleton until he understood.

"You can't be serious."

"It's personal."

"Hanley didn't send you."

"Hanley follows the rules. You broke the rules."

"You son of a bitch—"

But Devereaux showed him the pistol then and he cut himself off.

"This is murder."

"Yes," Devereaux said. "In cold blood. Without any redeeming aspects. Except you'll disappear from the face of the earth, which is reason enough."

Pendleton stared at the pistol.

"You gonna shoot me."

"If I have to," Devereaux said. "But I'll bet you can't make it to those trees across there."

"That's a bog."

"Swamp. Bog. Something like that."

"You know this place."

Devereaux said, "I know this place."

"You can't kill me."

"Go ahead."

"I won't go."

"Then I'll shoot you now, you son of a bitch."

The headlights illuminated the dark scene and sticks of trees across a marshy, long grass field. Pendleton licked the sweat from his upper lip.

"I can go away," Pendleton said. "You want that deal?"

"You're going away. That deal's been made."

Pendleton looked at him a long time, the blue eyes smoldering and careful at the same time.

"You're crazy, ain't you?" Pendleton said.

Devereaux made a signal. Pendleton sighed and opened the door of the car. The two men got out. The night air was close and the smell of rain was overwhelming. It would be raining very soon on a shuttered dark night by the Chesapeake Bay.

"I ain't done you a wrong, boy," Pendleton suddenly burst out.

"You did me a wrong a long time ago. In Paris and Zurich. You set me up for Kurt Heinemann. Kurt gave you a leg up the ladder, gave you names of Russian networks in Europe and you were the bright boy in Section. Oh, yes. You had to sacrifice a Section agent along the way named Devereaux but those things happen."

Devereaux's voice surprised him. It was calm but there was such a note of underlying hatred and contempt that both men were fascinated by it. The silence underscored it. The black night around them pressed the point to them.

"Whatever happened in Europe happened a long time ago, Devereaux."

"I didn't need revenge for that. I needed to be let alone. But you can't pull one wing off a butterfly without pulling off the other, can you? You wanted to set up Heinemann inside CI and you needed me to distract Mickey Connors long enough to get the code machine. So you rigged up dirty shit about Rita Macklin because it could force me to do what you wanted—"

"All that's been destroyed, Devereaux, you know that—"

"You made me expendable again. And Rita Macklin. And that poor dope in Hawaii who was disemboweled by the Japanese gang because he tried to be a good friend and reporter. . . . All the deaths come out of your hand."

"You have deaths on you, Devereaux. Nobody escapes clean."

"You dirtied Section. You set me up twice. You tried to use Rita Macklin. You're sitting in that house in Georgetown now, figuring how to get around Hanley, get around me. You broke the rules, Pendleton, and you're bad into your bones."

"You make this personal," Pendleton said.

Devereaux was silent. Then he nodded. "Personal," he said.

"You gonna shoot me?"

"You can run or I can shoot you. It doesn't matter, Pendleton. Maybe you could make the trees."

Pendleton stared in fear at the field. Then he began to run, the tall grass slowing him, slapping his face with stems, the muck pulling at his shoes. The muck accumulated around his shoes and it was under him, drawing him down. He cried then, not Devereaux's name or Hanley's. "Clothilde!" It was the cry of a name from his past; he was drowning in the earth growing up to his chest. *"Clothilde, aidez-moi!"*

Devereaux stared at the figure in the headlights sinking deeper into the sea of tall grass. His arms were above his head and he was clutching at the air.

"Clothilde!"

What memory was suddenly shaken in him?

210

Devereaux stared. The man's arms fell. And then his head sank beneath the grass and he cried and then it was muffled and then it was gone. The night was returned to insects and owls and the scurrying sounds of small animals. Devereaux stood still and waited and heard nothing but these other sounds of the busy Maryland night.

Then he got back into the car. He backed up the dirt path and found a turnaround. His rear wheels almost stuck once in the perpetually wet grass. It was a good night. It would rain and wash everything down and the tracks would be turned to rivers and smoothed out along with everything else.

On the highway, he drove slowly, thoughtfully. No one would speak of Pendleton's disappearance. Not officially. Hanley would ask him about it as a matter of routine and, in any case, would not believe him.

He parked the car in a far lot at Dulles and put his shoes in a paper bag that contained clean shoes. He put the clean shoes on and then took the bag to a garbage can and dumped them in. The car might sit in the far parking lot for a week before its theft was reported.

He went to the terminal building and took a limousine home, all the way to Bethesda. The ride cost eighty-five dollars and he left a ten-dollar tip.

He entered the apartment and she was asleep and he did not want to wake her. He went into the kitchen and poured himself a glass of vodka. He did not feel clean or free. He felt the weight of a man's death the way he felt other weights. The vodka startled him because he rarely drank it anymore and the taste of it reminded him of his times alone when he had been the secret agent in a foreign land, doing the little jobs of the trade, unable to share the terrible exile with anyone, unable to share the secret horrors that filled his heart. He had shared it with his vodka, inviting the numbness.

It was a night to feel nothing.

211

The rain was heavy when it came and it blotted out the secrets of the world for a time and it soothed him, sitting alone at a kitchen counter in this little place that was home. It made him think of other days, the rain and the vodka and the silence.

Other days.

THIRTY

Kevin Flick entered Dougherty's and nodded at the bartender who nodded back. The big man strode to the back and opened the door without knocking.

"Whatever happened, nobody knows nothing. Pendleton is just gone."

"It was Devereaux," Mickey Connors said. He had the bottle of Black Bush out and he was drinking shots. His eyes were steady, amused, but there was something else in them. "I figured Devereaux wrong. I could have helped him, couldn't I, Kevin?"

"You couldn't trust him."

"Ah, true, true." He stared at the bottle and the shot glass of amber liquid. "It's a sad thing not to trust in the world. You get weary sometimes and you want a hidey-hole where you can pull up and hide out the world for a while with someone. I could trust Maude. Twenty years she gave me and it was nothing but trust." He twisted the gold band on his finger. "Trust. You'll get married yerself, Kevin."

"I like things fine now. I got a girl or two. I don't need much more than that."

"But what you gotta have is what you find when you're looking for it." Mickey Connors shook his head. "And that girl. A red-hair. Always run with a red-hair, they're wild and they might do anything but if you find one you can trust, then you've found the best thing in the world. Do you suppose Devereaux knows he found it? What a lucky man he is?"

"I dunno," Kevin said. He stared at Mickey.

"Take a pew, Kevin. Have a glass."

Kevin poured whiskey in a glass and made a salute with it to the older man.

"He was lucky in her. She did the right thing by him, lad. She saved his fuckin' life, is all she did." Tasted a big gulp.

"That's the hell of it," Mickey said, shaking his head. He was looking at things in his mind but his eyes were on the bottle of whiskey on the desk.

"What is?"

"Maude. Rita Macklin. The way things turn out."

Kevin frowned. "I don't get it, Mickey."

"Luck, lad," Mickey Connors said. "The hell of it is that it's all luck in the end anyway."